HOPE DEFERRED

ELIZABETH MADDREY

OTHER BOOKS BY ELIZABETH MADDREY

Hope Ranch Series

Hope for Christmas

Peacock Hill Romance Series

A Heart Restored

A Heart Reclaimed

A Heart Realigned

Arcadia Valley Romance – Baxter Family Bakery Series

Loaves & Wishes

Muffins & Moonbeams

Cookies & Candlelight

Donuts & Daydreams

The 'Operation Romance' Series

Operation Mistletoe

Operation Valentine

Operation Fireworks

Operation Back-to-School

The 'Taste of Romance' Series

A Splash of Substance

A Pinch of Promise

A Dash of Daring

A Handful of Hope

A Tidbit of Trust

The 'Grant Us Grace' Series

Joint Venture

Wisdom to Know

Courage to Change

Serenity to Accept

Pathway to Peace

The 'Remnants' Series:

Faith Departed

Hope Deferred

Love Defined

Stand alone novellas

Kinsale Kisses: An Irish Romance

Luna Rosa (part of A Tuscan Legacy)

Non-Fiction

A Walk in the Valley: Christian encouragement for your journey through infertility

For the most recent listing of all my books, please visit my website.

©2016 by Elizabeth R.R. Maddrey

Hope Deferred, Second Edition

Hope Deferred First Edition©2014 by Elizabeth R.R. Maddrey, published by HopeSprings Books

Scripture quoted by permission. Quotations designated (NIV) are from THE HOLY BIBLE: NEW INTERNATIONAL VERSION®. NIV®. Copyright © 1973, 1978, 1984 by Biblica. All rights reserved worldwide.

Cover design by Marion Ueckermann

Published in the United States of America by Elizabeth Maddrey

Publisher's Note: This novel is a work of fiction. Names, characters, places, and incidents are either products of the author's imagination or used fictitiously. All characters are fictional, and any similarity to people living or dead is purely coincidental.

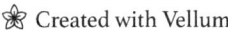 Created with Vellum

Hope deferred makes the heart sick,
But a longing fulfilled is a tree of life. –Proverbs 13:12

For all who are still waiting on the fulfillment of their longings.

1

"I've done all I can." Dr. Strong tented her fingers.

June swallowed the lump in her throat. It wasn't a surprise, not really. But the verdict still left her breathless. "So now what?"

"You'll want to find a reproductive endocrinologist. I'll make a copy of your file for you, hopefully that'll keep you from having to re-do three cycles of Clomid before moving on to something more likely to work."

June nodded. If only it was really that easy. She couldn't just go to an RE. Even with a referral from Dr. Strong, her insurance was going to fight it. And if they didn't pay...would Toby even consider it?

"Do you have someone you recommend?"

Dr. Strong shook her head. "Not really. It's not my specialty —and different insurance companies cover different medical groups. You tell me who your policy is most likely to work with and I'll write the referral to them."

"That's easy. No one." June huffed out a breath. "Sorry. I'll have to read through everything again, but I'm fairly sure they're not going to cover anything."

"Then I'd recommend choosing someone whose office is easy to get to first thing in the morning. You'll be making daily, or at least every other day, visits for ultrasounds during treatment." The doctor tapped a pen against her desk. "Tell you what, I'm going to fill out the form but leave the practice name blank. That way, once you decide where you're going, you can just fill it in. Saves you another office visit with me."

"Thanks." June watched as Dr. Strong scribbled on a pad of paper. How was she going to convince Toby?

JUNE'S HEAD fell back against the top of her desk chair. Why couldn't insurance companies just write in plain English? Her pulse throbbed in her temples and words continued to swim in front of her eyes, despite the fact that she was no longer looking at her computer screen. Her eyelids drifted shut. At least...at least what? Her mind went blank. Surely there were blessings to count somewhere?

"There she is, my beautiful bride." Toby's lips brushed across her forehead.

"Hi, sweetie. How was your day?" June flicked her eyes to the computer screen—it had gone blank. Thank goodness for screen savers. The conversation about medical treatment to start a family could wait for a little while. At least until she got her thoughts together.

"Eh." He shrugged. "You know how it is. How was your day off?"

Or maybe it couldn't wait. "Fine...I had a consultation with Dr. Strong."

Toby ran a hand through his hair. "Oh?"

"Yeah. I should have mentioned it—meant to, in fact—I just never figured out how. Then I thought it'd just be easier to tell you once I knew what she had to say. I'm sorry."

He sank into his chair and leaned forward, elbows on his knees. "Okay. I guess. So what did she say?"

June sighed. It was better to rip the band-aid off, right? "She can't do anything else for us. It's time to see a specialist if we're going to keep trying."

Toby nodded but said nothing.

June watched him. What was he thinking? The wheels were spinning behind his eyes, but his expression stayed blank. "We don't have to talk about it now. Or even do anything about it right away."

"How are you doing?"

June drew her eyebrows together. He wasn't mad that she'd forgotten to mention the appointment? Or that they were going to have to pay for this out of pocket? "Um...okay, I guess. Disappointed. But I'm honestly starting to get used to that. This last year has left a layer of discouragement over most of my life that's thicker than the dust on the bookshelves."

The corner of Toby's mouth quirked up. "Is that a hint that I need to dust more?"

"You know what I mean."

"So, just disappointed?"

What was he getting at? "Not *just*, no. But I haven't sorted through everything yet—processed it, I guess. I...honestly, I was more worried that you were going to be angry."

He rolled his chair closer to hers and took her hand. "I'm sorry."

"There's nothing for you to be sorry about. As far as we know, all our problems are my fault. If anyone needs to be sorry, it's me. I know you didn't sign on for a broken wife."

He squeezed her hand. "That's not what I meant—and you're not broken. But we'll come back to that." He cleared his throat and waited until their eyes met. "I'm sorry that I've made you feel like you can't—or shouldn't—talk to me about this. I don't want you to only worry that I'm going to be angry when you're hurting."

"Oh." June offered a slight smile. "Thanks."

"I love you. Kids or no kids. When I asked you to marry me, I signed on to be your husband and spend the rest of my life with you. Anything else is gravy." He stood and kissed her forehead. "Why don't I see what I can scrounge for dinner? Then afterward, we can tackle the nightmare of the insurance website and see what we can figure out."

June's mouth dropped open as he left the room. He was taking this so well...had her impressions from the last four months been that far off? After their first failed cycle on Clomid in April, he'd been so insistent that they wait until June to try again. Then when that cycle failed, he'd pushed for another break before a third try. She'd assumed he was going to want an even longer break now that he was going to have to be more actively involved in the process. Maybe he didn't understand how much more he was going to have to do? Even if he didn't, she was going to savor having him back on her side for as long as it lasted.

JUNE EASED out from under the covers. Toby's breathing continued its even rhythm, punctuated by quiet whuffles every fourth breath. He was so cute. He probably wouldn't appreciate the term, but it was what fit. Especially when he was asleep. Careful to avoid the squeaky floorboards, she made her way downstairs to the office and wiggled her computer mouse.

The time they'd spent looking at insurance and various fertility doctors after dinner hadn't been particularly productive. Insurance wasn't going to cover anything after testing. That was clear. The tests themselves were likely to be covered, at least the way they were reading the coverage descriptions. But it wasn't clear if a specialist could do the testing or if she had to convince Dr. Strong to do it.

Sighing, June clicked on Solitaire. The cards darted across the screen into neat piles. Why couldn't life be that easy? Click a button, get a nice, manageable stack of things to deal with and tick through them one at a time. She dragged a few cards around before closing the unfinished game and opening a browser. Automatically, she clicked the Facebook button. Maybe someone had posted something funny that would penetrate the hazy funk that had settled over her as she got ready for bed and was responsible for this bout of insomnia.

Or not. The first item in her newsfeed was a baby picture from Ginger and Martin. She quickly scrolled past. It wasn't that their daughter was ugly—she was beautiful—but she was also one more kick in the gut. At least she wasn't Facebook friends with everyone in the small group. The August baby-boom had made the class almost unbearable. Having it thrust in her face every time she ventured online would've simply capped off the misery.

She was about to close the browser when her chat box popped up and the computer dinged.

What are you doing up?

June glanced at the time and shook her head.

I could ask you the same thing, Lydia. Couldn't sleep. U?

She reopened solitaire as she waited for Lydia to respond.

Same here. Thinking too much, mostly. You free for coffee anytime soon?

Her head fell back and she stared at the ceiling. Was she free for coffee? The easy answer was yes. Her social calendar wasn't bustling and never had been. But her relationship with Lydia had been weird since April. Relationships with a lot of people had been weird since April. On the other hand, Toby had a guy's night planned for Friday, and July and Gareth were going away for the weekend. Coffee with Lydia would be better than hanging around the house moping.

Friday night?

It's a date! Guess I should run and try to sleep. You should too.

She closed the browser and stared at the photo of her and Toby grinning from the desktop. Sleep. Sure. Like that was going to happen.

2

June stepped off the escalator at the Metro station and paused to get her bearings. She and Lydia had finally decided to meet at one of the coffee-slash-sandwich shops that lined the streets of Arlington. Since it was just a few blocks from her office, June had left her car in the garage rather than risk not finding a closer street spot. Judging from the number of people bustling along the sidewalk and the cars creeping in both directions, that had been a good decision.

She wove through the crowds, pausing at the corner before darting through the stopped traffic against the light. She, and the handful of people who followed, earned a few honks, but it wasn't as if the cars had anywhere to go. She tugged open the cafe door and inhaled. They either really did bake their bread on the premises or they'd found a fantastic air freshener. Her gaze roamed over the seating areas. No Lydia. Was she early? A quick glance at her watch confirmed that she was actually about ten minutes late. Whatever. She'd get a coffee and then stake a claim on one of the cushy chairs. Even if Lydia didn't show, she'd have a nice evening out of the house.

Mug in one hand and metal table stand holding her order

number in the other, June slid into one of the two remaining leather chairs tucked in the back corner. She propped her foot on the other chair and set the number on the round table angled between them. She blew across the top of her mug before sipping. Chocolate and whipped cream danced across her taste buds, a hint of vanilla sneaking in as she swallowed. Perfection.

Lydia dropped several shopping bags on the floor. "I'm sorry I'm late. I got caught up at the mall searching for stuff to send with a friend who's leaving for the mission field soon."

"Don't worry about it. I decided if you stood me up I was going to enjoy my coffee and dessert and do some people watching."

Lydia laughed. "Fat chance on me standing you up. I may be late, but I'll never ditch you, that's a promise. Friends are hard to come by these days. Let me run and order some coffee and I'll be right back."

June watched Lydia scurry across the café and shook her head. Where did she get that energy? A server with a precariously balanced tray paused and eyed the number on the table.

"I'll be right back with that."

"No problem."

Lydia made her way back just as the server returned with June's dessert.

"Oooh. That looks yummy."

June grinned. "I couldn't help myself. It's either going to be incredible or terrible—I don't think there's room for in-between with bread pudding made of flatbread."

"Well?" Lydia sipped her coffee as June took a bite.

"It's...interesting. Want a taste?"

Lydia frowned. "This isn't one of those tricks, like when you know the milk has gone bad and you try to sucker someone else into tasting it just to be sure, is it?"

June laughed. "Promise. It's not bad, it's just different."

Lydia gave June a long look before taking a bite. "Okay. I see what you mean. It's interesting."

June slid the plate onto the table. "Help yourself if you want more."

"I'm good. But thanks." Lydia took another long sip from her coffee. "So, how've you been?"

June shrugged. Of course they were going to get into things...but did it have to be the first topic of the night? Weren't you supposed to warm up with small talk first? "Good, I guess. What about you? How are things going after..."

"The miscarriage?" Lydia flashed a weak smile.

"Yeah."

"I'm doing all right. Kevin's still having a hard time with it though. We've actually backed away from trying for a while because of it." Lydia huffed out a breath. "And the next person who dismisses his pain because it was a 'chemical pregnancy' is going to get an earful."

June winced. "Sorry."

"No. I'm sorry. You haven't done anything. It's just frustrating because people seem to think that calling it a chemical pregnancy somehow means I didn't lose a baby. But conception still took place—so really, how is it different? It was just a very early miscarriage. And it hit Kevin hard."

What did you say to that? When you laid it all out like that, June agreed...but she'd been guilty of thinking exactly the kinds of things Lydia described, particularly when comparing Lydia and July.

"I've killed all possibility of normal conversation now, haven't I? I've already sent the majority of my friends packing— or at least into hiding—with my tirade. Particularly the ones who have newborns and are feeling awkward about that. And I was hoping..." Lydia frowned and started to stand.

"Wait. You're fine." June grabbed Lydia's hand and tugged

until she sat back down. "I'm sorry that I didn't realize what you were going through."

Lydia sagged back into the chair. "Why would you? I've been trying to put on a happy face. The last thing I want is people feeling like they have the right to say I deserved this because of my past. And you know people are going there. Thankfully, so far at least, they haven't been doing it to my face. Anyway, enough about me. Tell me what's been going on with you? You've been really scarce at church lately."

June filled Lydia in on their failed attempts with Clomid and the doctor's latest pronouncement. "So now, we're going to have to figure out how to choose a fertility doctor and how we're supposed to pay for any visits we make to them."

"Ouch."

"Pretty much. I don't have all the details yet, but if you Google infertility costs...it doesn't paint a pretty picture. So when you throw that into the mix, it really means you need to choose your doctor well. But how do you do that? It isn't as if you can walk up to every woman with a child and say, 'Hi. Did you conceive with medical assistance? Would you recommend your doctor?'"

Lydia chuckled.

"I know—but what else do you do? If you needed something like a podiatrist, that's exactly what you'd do. It's just so frustrating." June sighed and spun her empty mug in her hands.

"I might actually have an idea." Lydia rummaged in her purse. She pulled out her phone and began tapping. "Karin, the person taking the stuff I bought tonight with her to Mexico, used to work in the NICU. She might have some ideas."

June frowned. "Why? What does the NICU have to do with anything?"

Lydia shrugged. "Maybe nothing. But I'm thinking NICU often equals multiples and multiples equal assisted reproduction. At least some of the time. So maybe in her time there she ran into the doctors—or at least heard something from the parents."

"I guess it's worth a shot. Though everything I've read says that the RE passes you off to your regular OB when you're through the first trimester."

"Well, then maybe not. But it can't hurt to ask. And if she wants more details, I'll just say it's for me. It isn't like having a recommendation for a doctor is ever a bad idea. Now tell me why you haven't been in small group. I miss seeing you."

JUNE DROPPED her purse on the kitchen island and kicked her shoes into the corner. Meeting with Lydia had been exactly what she'd needed. She'd been letting the baby boom in the small group keep her from enjoying the friends she did have there. That had to stop.

As they were saying goodbye at the Metro, Lydia's friend had come through with two names of doctors she'd liked. Neither one was familiar. June pulled the napkin from her pocket and smoothed it out. She might as well go look them up now since Toby wasn't home yet. Ignoring the flashing light on the answering machine, she went to the office and flopped into her chair. What was the likelihood that a recommended doctor actually took their insurance?

When the website finally loaded, happy parents with babies slid across the screen, each photo singing the praises of the doctors at the clinic. June's stomach clenched. Sure, having a child was the goal, but didn't they realize those photos made it hard to even look at their website? They were probably stock photos anyway. She clicked on "About Us" and began reading, checking the doctor names against the note she'd scrawled as

Lydia rattled off the names. Both doctors worked for the same practice. Was that good or bad?

"I'M surprised you're still up."

June jolted. "Sheesh. Way to sneak up on someone."

Toby chuckled and leaned down, planting a kiss on her cheek. "What're you looking at?"

She rubbed her eyes. Somehow she'd managed to spend two hours reading through the doctor's website. "Lydia has a friend who's a nurse who recommended this reproductive endo-crinology practice. I was just going to look up what insurance they worked with and maybe explore a little of their philosophy, but I got caught up on the client testimonials."

He raised his eyebrows. "And?"

She shrugged. "I don't know. It's not like they put anything negative on their website. It sounds like it's wonderful, but maybe the next thing to do is a search on the doctor's name— or even the practice—and see what else pops up. There's probably someone with something negative to say out there."

"Isn't that just going to be people with an axe to grind if they're not on the testimonial page?"

"Probably. But that's just the opposite spectrum of what they put in all their marketing materials. The truth is probably somewhere in the middle."

Toby grabbed her hand and tugged. "Come to bed. Maybe we'll end up not needing to find out."

3

July scanned the crowded sidewalks. Where was her sister? She squeezed the top of the paper bag holding her lunch then forced her fingers to relax and smooth out the wrinkles. She caught the barest flash of dark hair and bright colors. That had to be June.

"Hey, 'Julie-bird.' Sorry. Someone higher up must be on Bob's case. This is the fourth all-hands meeting he's called in the last week. And he's really not saying anything we don't already know. I don't understand what's going on. They're probably reorganizing. Again."

July shook her head. "Didn't they reorganize in May?"

"Yep. But the guy they put over Bob should never have been hired, let alone put in charge. Those of us who actually listened in his first talking-head meeting figured that out. I think the powers-that-be are finally piecing it together. We've lost four proposals in the last four months."

"Ouch." July winced. "I'm so glad I'm not in contract work."

"But you are, kind of. You have people clamoring for you to handle their accounting needs. We have to go beg people to let us write their software."

She had a point. And they did, occasionally, lose clients to other firms. But it was rare. And usually only when the accountant was also changing firms.

"Anyway. How was your weekend? And why aren't you eating yet?" June tucked one leg under the other and slumped against the back of the bench.

"Where's your lunch?" July twisted the top of her lunch bag.

"Not hungry. But you eat."

She narrowed her eyes. 'Not hungry' was becoming too common a theme for her sister these days. Should she say something? A possible conversation played in her head, culminating in an argument and her sister storming off. Yeah...probably better to keep quiet. With a final frown at her sister, July pulled a sandwich and a bunch of grapes from her bag and set them on the bench between them.

"Feel free to graze." July picked up half the sandwich and took a bite. "As for my weekend, it wasn't anything special. Gareth spent most of Saturday raking in the backyard. I don't really see the point. Half the trees haven't even started dropping their leaves, and won't until close to the end of October. But he says it's good to stay on top of things. I think he's just trying to avoid another conversation about kids."

June angled her head to one side. "He still won't talk about it?"

"Nope. If I try to mention anything, he either storms off or treats me like an imbecile. I mean, I get that the ectopic was scary. I was there. But I have one healthy tube and the doctor seems positive that I should be able to conceive and carry to full term without any problem. Although..." July moistened her lips with the tip of her tongue.

"Although?"

She cleared her throat. "Doc Granger did suggest working with a reproductive endocrinologist. Apparently, they have a broader range of tests—physical and hormonal—for women with recurrent losses. And since they monitor you so closely, they might be able to head some problems off at the pass. Plus, with only one tube, it probably makes sense to have that monitoring just for the sake of maximizing our chances as far as timing goes."

June nodded. "What does Gareth say?"

July's shoulders fell. "I haven't been able to even get that much out before he starts arguing that he's not risking my life for the chance at a child. I don't know what to do."

"Want me to have Toby talk to him?"

Did she? It was an appealing suggestion. But how would Gareth respond? He'd know she'd been talking to June— though he'd probably assumed she was doing that already. And so what if she was? Hadn't last year proved that keeping secrets from her twin wasn't the way to operate?

"I don't know. Maybe you could ask Toby if he thinks it's a good idea? I feel like I'm walking on eggshells—I don't like it."

"I know that feeling. I'll run it by him, see what he thinks. In the meantime, maybe it'll give you some ammunition to know we're going for a consultation with Dr. DiCola at NatCap Fertility on Friday."

"Wow...I guess I didn't realize you were moving in that direction already."

"Dr. Strong told me last week there was nothing more she was comfortable doing. The Clomid failed so...it's either a reproductive endocrinologist or give up. I'm not ready to do that yet, so we're going to have a consult. I'm not sure how much further it'll go though. Our insurance covers basically nothing and, of course, when we set up the flexible spending last year we didn't have this in mind."

"How'd you choose someone? I've been looking online and it's overwhelming. There are so many options out there."

June snickered. "Tell me about it. Lydia asked a friend who was a NICU nurse if she had any recommendations.

This is who she came back with. So...we'll see. The online reviews are mixed. But I suspect any doctor is going to have people who love them and hate them, depending on how things go."

July nodded, lips pursed. "Keep me in the loop, would you? One of Gareth's strongest objections is that we can't just throw a dart to choose a doctor for something like this. Maybe knowing that you're seeing the same people would help him at least think about it."

JULY SET her bulging briefcase at the foot of the stairs and slipped out of her heels. Stooping to scoop them up, she trudged up to the bedroom. She had three clients who had finally sent all the information she needed to file their income taxes. With just about a month until their filing extension ended, it was going to be a rush to get them done and turned in. At least when she brought work home she could work in her pajamas. Gareth would be annoyed, but it wasn't as if she couldn't sit on the couch with him and work while he watched TV.

She sighed and dropped her shoes in the closet before shrugging out of her suit jacket and carefully hanging it alongside her slacks. She flicked her gaze to the bed. Wouldn't it be lovely to stretch out for just a few minutes? Her muscles loosened at the thought and she sank into the mattress. She wouldn't fall asleep. She was just going to relax for a minute, maybe five. Then she'd get up and fix supper and get back to work. Rolling to her side, she pillowed her head on her arms with a deep sigh.

"Long day?"

"I'm not asleep." July yawned and swiped a hand over her eyes.

"Of course not." Gareth kissed her nose. "Want me to order takeout?"

"Mmm. That'd be nice. I have a steak I was going to make you grill, but it'll keep 'til tomorrow. What time is it?"

"Just after seven."

July bolted to a sitting position. "Seriously?"

"Yep. Why?"

She groaned. "That's an hour of work I could have gotten done."

Gareth chuckled. "Lazy bones."

"Whatever. Go order dinner, I'll be down in a minute." She shook her head as Gareth began whistling, the off-key notes floating up the stairs behind him. An hour. Even with the work she needed to do, she'd also wanted to spend a few minutes looking up NatCap Fertility. She'd do a better job convincing Gareth they should at least go talk to someone if she knew more about the place, and it wasn't something she wanted in her browser history at work.

After splashing water on her face, she went down to the living room, stopping to grab her work bag along the way.

"What'd you order?" She settled onto the couch next to Gareth and began unloading client files and her laptop.

"Chinese. We had pizza at work today. Didn't feel like having it two meals in a row."

"Fair enough. How's everything going with your research?"

Gareth tipped his head to the side, his eyes on her. "You really want to know?"

July drew her brows together. "Of course I do. Why would you even ask that?"

He shrugged. "You haven't asked lately. The few times I've mentioned anything I've gotten the distracted uh-huh that tells me you weren't actually listening. Figured you'd gotten bored with the details."

Her hands stilled on the keys of her laptop and she swiveled to face him, their knees touching. "I'm sorry. I..." Was now the time to bring it up? She didn't want to start another fight, but they'd been talking past each other for awhile now. She sighed. "We need to talk—really talk—about kids."

His whole body stiffened. "What does that have to do with anything?"

"Everything. This," she gestured to his posture, "isn't okay. I've heard chapter and verse on how you feel. But anytime I try to talk, you cut me off. I know you're scared. I'd be lying if I said I wasn't too. The difference is I still want to try."

"Jules..."

She grabbed his hand. "I want to have children with you, Gar. I want to celebrate who we are as a couple, make a family, and know that there will be future generations because of our love."

"And if those future generations have to grow up without a mother? You're okay with that?"

"No, of course not. But have you actually looked at how likely that is?" June frowned. It was the same argument they'd been having all summer. Nothing ever changed. How was it supposed to unless they got some new information?

"Even if the odds are one in a million, what if you're that one?" Gareth stood and shoved his hands into his pockets as he paced across the room. "What then? I'm supposed to comfort myself with the fact that I lost my wife and my child lost his mother on the slimmest margin possible?"

Her shoulders sagged and she took a deep breath. "But what if I'm *not* that one? I don't want to spend the rest of my life regretting not looking into how realistic that worst case scenario really is. Do you?"

Gareth started to speak several times before his jaw snapped shut. The doorbell rang and he stalked from the room.

Great. Just great. July's head flopped against the back of the couch. Now they'd have three days of awkward silence as they both tried to avoid saying anything to set the other off. And in all their conversation, and there'd be plenty of that, they'd not manage to actually say anything. She could apologize...but why? All she'd done is try to get him to understand her perspective.

Gareth returned with two steaming plates of food. He set one on the coffee table in front of her and grabbed the TV remote before sitting with his own.

"I'm tired of this, Gareth. We need to see someone. Either a doctor to explore our options for having a baby or Pastor Brown for marriage counseling." July stood and grabbed her work bag and the plate of food. "Let me know what you decide."

4

Wait. What? Her words were a punch in his gut. Gareth's jaw dropped as he watched July collect her things and not-quite-storm from the room. So his choice was to get more information on how he could possibly lose his wife due to medical complications because she insisted on trying to have children even though the last year had pretty conclusively shown that was a bad idea. Or they could go to marriage counseling...he scrubbed his hands over his face. How had they ended up here? Hadn't she been paying attention this last year? Didn't she get how close to dying she'd been?

He stared at the TV for several minutes before clicking it off. What was he supposed to do? He looked down at the plate of food in his lap. His stomach twisting, he carried the plate into the kitchen and set it on the counter. Maybe he'd be able to eat it later.

Tucking his hands in his pockets, he went looking for July. She wasn't in the office or the dining room. Frowning, he headed upstairs and poked his head into their bedroom. Where had she gone? He eyed the closed door of the guest bedroom.

Why would she be in there? And since she was—she had to be, there was nowhere else in the house for her to be—should he leave her alone or force the issue?

He glared at the door and finally raised his hand to knock, stopping just before his knuckles connected. This was his house too, he wasn't going to knock. And she needed to talk to him. She couldn't just make ultimatums and leave the room. Heat washed through him and he wrenched the door open.

July sat cross-legged on the bed, stacks of papers spread around her, her computer balanced on her knees. She looked up from her laptop.

"July." He leaned against the door frame and cleared his throat. "Clearly, we need to talk."

"What do you think I've been trying to do for the last three months? I'm tired of trying to talk to you. It's evident you're not interested in listening." She pulled a stack of papers closer to her and flipped the top page.

"Can you stop for a minute?"

"Not really." Her hands stilled on the keyboard and her head fell to the side as she looked up at him. "I've got three clients here whose extension on their income tax runs out next month. I never seem to have the time to deal with the small clients when I'm at work because the corporate clients take up every minute. And frankly…I don't want to rehash our argument yet again, unless it's in front of someone who's actually going to listen when I speak."

"I am listening." He'd been listening the whole time, but it probably wasn't a good idea to mention that just now. "Just because I don't agree doesn't mean I'm not listening."

She pulled her lower lip between her teeth and gave a slow nod. "Fine. But in all your 'listening', I don't think you've heard me."

What did that mean? He drew his eyebrows together. "How

can you say that? I know you want children. I get that. But I don't think you're considering all the possible ramifications…"

"Just stop." She pushed her fingers through her hair. "I'm not doing this right now. I've spent too long trying to make you understand and all you do is belittle my ability to grasp the situation. I've told you where I stand. Now would you please go away and let me do my work?"

"Bu…" Gareth snapped off his response. She'd buried herself back in her work, and from her posture he wasn't going to get her attention again anytime soon. He swallowed the bile rising in his throat and turned. He paused, one hand on the doorknob. "I love you, July."

She didn't look up. Frowning, Gareth pulled the door closed with a soft click. Had he just lost his wife because he was trying too hard not to lose her?

JULY HADN'T COME to bed. At ten, he'd knocked on the door and received an unintelligible grunt in response. That hadn't encouraged him to peek in and ask if she'd be coming soon. So he'd waited. The light under the guest room door had glowed into the hallway until midnight. After it turned off, he'd waited for July for another fifteen minutes. Then he'd switched off the bedroom light and tried to sleep.

By three, he'd given up. He was going to be staring at the ceiling for the rest of the night. He could get up and…what? Go in to work? He wouldn't be able to get into the lab—not that any of his experiments would be finished yet anyway. They all needed a minimum of twelve-hours between observations, and he set them up to run overnight to avoid downtime during the day. He could catch up on paperwork, but he wasn't actually behind. The nature of his experiments meant he had downtime, and he tried to get as much done as he could so he didn't have to drag it home. He could read. Or turn on the TV.

He sighed and rolled to his side. None of that held any interest. What he wanted to do was go shake July awake and get this figured out. But was that even possible at this point? Neither of the options she'd given him was great. What would Pastor Brown say if they showed up in his office? Gareth ran through the usual points of their argument, trying to put himself in Pastor Brown's head. Was he being unreasonable? Would it hurt anything to have a doctor look at their history? Surely a medical professional would side with Gareth after they understood that July coming out of the whole thing alive was more important than anything else.

Of course, July would disagree with that statement. She was perfectly content to die in the quest for a child. Well, maybe not perfectly content. But she certainly never seemed to understand that he wasn't ever going to volunteer to be a heartbroken single-dad. His muscles tensed. He'd faced the reality of losing July in the spring...he couldn't go there again. Gareth flopped onto his back and pillowed his head on his arm. Why couldn't she understand that?

What was he missing? There had to be something for her to continue to be so upset with him. He wanted children too—she knew that, didn't she? But there were other ways to have a family without putting her life at risk. Had he ever actually mentioned that to her? He frowned, thinking through their conversations. Everything seemed to derail and turn into an argument before that option came up. Was that his fault? Probably. Just the thought of losing her sent his pulse into overdrive. He sighed. There wasn't any point in trying to bring it up now. He'd only seen July this mad—or determined—once before. He was going to have to choose one of her options. Soon.

5

"Dr. DiCola will be right with you." The young woman in scrubs smiled and pulled the door shut.

June looked around the room and fought a shiver. Diplomas adorned the entire wall behind the imposing cherry desk. The other walls were lined with bookshelves that overflowed with thick medical texts. Files and books lay in orderly stacks on a credenza in front of the window. Two leather chairs faced the desk. There weren't any personal trinkets anywhere. She swallowed and glanced at Toby from the corner of her eye. Did he think it felt as impersonal as she did?

"Might as well sit. I guess." Toby slid his fingers through hers as he lowered himself into one of the chairs.

"Okay. Right." June took a deep breath and sat, clutching her purse in her lap. "How long do you think..."

There was a brisk knock at the door as it swung open.

"Hi. How are you? I'm Dr. DiCola." The short man looked to be in his early forties. Thick black hair was parted in a razor-sharp line on one side of his scalp, swept across, and held in place with visible quantities of hair gel. He extended his hand to June and Toby in turn before rounding the desk and sitting. He steepled his fingers and offered a perfunctory smile. "What brings you here today?"

June looked at Toby. He gave a slight nod. Great. She was up. She cleared her throat.

"Um. We've been trying to get pregnant a little over a year now. We've done three cycles of Clomid with my regular doctor without any result. So...she said there wasn't anything else she was comfortable doing."

Dr. DiCola pursed his lips. "Have you had any tests done?"

"They ran some blood work. But nothing other than that." June pulled her lower lip between her teeth. Hadn't Dr. Strong's office sent the records over like she'd asked?

"I thought Dr. Strong was sending over the records." Toby frowned, looking first at June, then the doctor. "Didn't you get them?"

"Oh, probably." Dr. DiCola gave an airy wave toward the stacks of folders on the credenza. "I just always like to hear it from the patients themselves. Once we've worked out a basic treatment plan, I'll look over those records and see if there's anything else I need to know."

Shouldn't it be the other way around? June looked over at Toby. A slight frown was etched on his face, but he said nothing. "Okay?"

Dr. DiCola slid a notepad off his desk and began to draw. "Basically we have two options. There's intrauterine insemination, or IUI, and in vitro fertilization, IVF. Since you've done three cycles with Clomid, there's really no point trying any more of that. And, since you haven't appeared to conceive, it's unlikely that a natural cycle—where we just help monitor your cycle without drugs to maximize timing—would be any use."

He continued to draw for a minute, then flipped the pad of paper so she and Toby could see it. "We're going to want to do a pelvic ultrasound, and hysterosalpingogram, plus a bit more bloodwork than your doctor probably did. Have you had a glucose tolerance test?"

June frowned. "No. Why would I need to?"

"Well, with someone your size, diabetes is a real concern. It's always better to know right off the bat if it's something we'll be dealing with."

June bristled. Yes, she'd gained weight. But she wasn't anywhere near the kind of weight that would bring on diabetes, was she? She gave a curt nod.

"The HSG will tell us if your tubes are clear. Then Toby will need to do a semen analysis, make sure everything's working fine on his end. Though, again, looking at your weight, it's very likely the problem, if there is one, is on your end."

Toby reached over and set his hand on her knee as she tensed. She swallowed back the retort on the tip of her tongue. It wouldn't do to alienate the doctor on their first visit.

"You'll get prescriptions for those tests at checkout. Which procedure did you think you wanted to do?"

"Could you give us a little more detail about how they each work?" Toby gave her knee a light squeeze.

"Of course." Dr. DiCola flipped to a new page on the notepad and began drawing as he explained the two procedures. There wasn't much difference between the two in the preliminary stages. The primary choice was between triggering ovulation and, essentially, injecting Toby's sperm and hoping conception would occur, or harvesting mature ova and fertilizing them in the lab, then implanting mature embryos after a couple of days.

"So we don't actually need to make a decision right now, right?" Toby reached for the sheet of paper the doctor extended.

"No. Not immediately. We can get started with the testing

and initial protocol. But you'll need to have a firm decision before the follicles start to mature so that we know how to proceed."

"Okay. We'll talk it over some more and have an answer at our next appointment." Toby glanced at June.

She nodded. That would work. If they were really going to keep working with this guy. His whole attitude made her skin crawl. Didn't Toby feel it? The condescension? Of course, he'd always been better at taking that in stride. She clamped her mouth shut and fought the urge to sigh.

"Any questions?" Dr. DiCola folded his hands on top of his desk.

"With IVF...are you willing to only harvest and fertilize a small number of eggs—say maybe three—so we're not creating babies that we have no intention of birthing?"

The doctor's lips thinned, edging into a scowl. "The success of IVF relies on having a large pool of *embryos* to choose from. If you insist on tying my hands, then yes, I'll work within those confines. But you have to understand that doing so increases your risk of failure. If we only create three embryos, you run the risk of having nothing worth transferring."

June shook her head. "What do you mean?"

"It's our practice to only transfer embryos that have a high probability of success, this is based on a number of factors. But if you only have three to choose from, you may not get any that are what we consider excellent. And there's very little point in transferring those as it's unlikely they'll implant."

"But..."

The doctor shook his head. "That's all getting ahead of things. We can discuss what gets transferred once we know what the embryos actually look like. For now, you just need to consider the fact that this proposal means you may need to do more than three rounds of IVF—and even then, your chances of success are not going to be in line with the percentages on our website. Your initial paperwork has all the standard explanations about that, but when you change up the protocol, we can't guarantee anything. Were there other questions?"

Hundreds of them swam in her mind, but June shook her head. No point making him angry before they'd even finished the initial paperwork.

"Great. Give this," the doctor pulled a sheet of paper from a standing file, "to the check out nurse. She'll get you the prescriptions you need. Once the tests are complete and we have those results, we'll schedule your next appointment."

June took the paper with a tight smile and grabbed the doorknob.

Toby put his hand on the small of her back. "Thanks so much."

"Do you feel like we just hopped onto an assembly line, or is it just me?" June snapped her seatbelt together.

Toby shook his head as he eased the car onto the busy Arlington streets. "What were you expecting? They do this for a living, and it's all they do. Of course they have a streamlined process."

Was that all it was? "I guess. It just felt so...impersonal. I mean, they're going to hopefully help us create a child. Shouldn't they think of us as more than a file number?"

Toby shrugged. "Sure, in a perfect world. But really, June, how many people do they see in a day? There were what, fifteen other people in the waiting room when we got there? And a whole different set by the time we left?"

He probably had a point. But why couldn't they see the same number of patients and still seem to care? Maybe it wouldn't matter.

"So, thoughts on the treatment plans?" Toby swung into the left lane and accelerated around a bus.

June pinched the bridge of her nose. "Too many. I guess I'm not completely convinced we need IUI. I don't understand why we couldn't just do the ovulation inducing drugs and monitoring and then make a baby the normal way. Is that just not something they do?"

"Huh. It's not something I'd thought of. Though I'll admit the only thought I've given any of it has been reading through the website to get as much information as I could. And the options they list online are the same as the ones he went over with us." Toby frowned, drumming his fingers on the steering wheel.

"I imagine it has to do with their success statistics. The more variables they control, the more likely it is we'll conceive and bump up their numbers, which in turn drives more business their way."

"Cynical. Probably not wrong, but still cynical." He flashed a grin.

"With the options he gave us, I'm really only comfortable with IUI. I can't get past the fact that with IVF, you're creating babies—but they throw them away so casually. Did you hear him? No point in transferring the less-than-excellent ones. And his emphasis on the word embryo, as if that somehow changes the fact that it's a living human being."

"Do you want to look around? Try someplace else and see if they have a different attitude?"

Did she? This was the doctor people recommended. After Lydia's initial mention, June had checked around. The few people she could find who knew someone who'd used a reproductive endocrinologist agreed that DiCola was one of the best. But maybe they'd be better off with less-than-the-best if it meant the doctor also had a heart for the babies that were being created. "I don't know. This whole thing...I pray and I pray for God to make it clear what we should do, how to proceed and there's nothing but deafening silence from Heaven. Seeing this doctor—any doctor—are we stepping out in faith or marching willfully out of God's plan? And how are we supposed to know if God remains mute?"

6

"How'd it go at the doctor?" Gareth closed the lid of the grill and hooked a deck chair with his foot, tugging it closer before he sat.

"Heard about that, did you?" Toby shook his head. "It was fine, I guess. June would disagree, but I'm still not sure what she was expecting. We went to a doctor's office. Have you ever gone to see a medical professional and left with a warm, fuzzy feeling?"

Gareth snickered. "As a medical professional, I'll admit that I bristle somewhat when you say that. But...that's why I'm in research, not practice."

"I don't know that I'd admit it to her, but the guy does seem pretty brusque. June started to ask a few questions about doing IVF in a way that's in line with a pro-life view of conception and he shut her down fast. Which pretty much means IVF is off the table. He said he'd do it our way if we forced him but..."

"He said those words?"

"Basically, yeah." Toby slid down in the chair and crossed his ankles.

"Nice. Real charmer."

Toby laughed. "Exactly. So now June's debating the finer points of IUI versus asking about doing ovulation induction with natural conception...and that's enough talk about our sex life for me. You?"

"Yeah, I'm good." Gareth shot a glance toward the kitchen and cleared his throat. "What's the longest you've been in a fight with June?"

"I dunno. Couple days? Even then it isn't as if we hadn't been trying to hash things out...why?" Even as he asked, Toby fought the urge to groan. Gareth had been his best friend for long enough that Toby knew it had to be serious if Gareth was bringing it up. And Toby had enough on his mind right now. Getting involved—even marginally—in a disagreement with his sister-in-law was just not something he wanted to do.

Everything about Gareth seemed to collapse in on itself. "She's been sleeping in the guest room since Monday."

"Dude." That was serious. He and June had had some fights. And there had been a few nights when one or the other of them might go to the couch. But five days? Nuh-uh.

"I know. I've tried to talk to her, but all she says is that she's given me my options." Gareth stuffed his hands into his pockets. "But the options suck."

"That might be the case, but you're going to have to make a choice if she's not willing to even talk until then. You can't let a disagreement go on like that, man. You know that."

"I just keep thinking she's going to come to her senses..."

"You mean see things your way, right?"

Gareth frowned. "Whose side are you on?"

Toby held up his hands. "Nobody's. I don't even know what you're arguing about. But what I do know is that this isn't healthy. If she won't talk about it, then you need to do what you can to get things started toward resolution."

"So, what? She makes ultimatums and I have to cave?" Gareth surged to his feet. "How is that right? She's holding our marriage hostage and I have to capitulate? Why shouldn't she be the one who has to back down from her stance? She's the one who's being unreasonable."

Toby watched his friend pace the length of the deck. How far into this did he want to get? Who was he kidding, he was already in it. At this point, he might as well go all in. "You have a point. I don't disagree. But how much is it worth? If you're both going to be too stubborn to bend, your relationship is going to break. Is that what you want?"

Gareth paused at the edge of the deck and stared out over the yard. "Of course not. But…"

"There are no 'but's. You need to do what it takes to fix things. It's gone on long enough. I'm not saying she's right, and I hope that once you get whatever this is settled you can talk about how this is not the way to handle arguments."

Gareth nodded.

What else should he say? Toby didn't want to know all the details, though June probably did. He wasn't going to ask her, either. Smoke billowing out of the grill lid caught his eye.

"Um, Gar? I think dinner might be on fire."

"That was an interesting evening."

Toby scoffed. "I was going to go with tense."

"That, too." June shook her head and disappeared into the closet. "Did you get details from Gareth?"

Toby stripped off his jeans and tossed them into the corner. "No. And I don't want them, either."

June poked her head out of the closet. "You say that like I'm desperate to get involved."

Like that was an unreasonable assumption. He kept the thought to himself and shrugged. "Sorry. I know you end up getting sucked into your sister's life, and most of the time you don't mind, but this seems like something where we need to keep our hands off."

Pulling her pajama top over her head, June crossed to the bathroom. "I don't disagree. It's hard, though. They're both being so..."

"Stubborn? Stupid?" Toby pulled back the covers and slid into bed. Maybe stupid was over the top. But how did you let a fight with your wife last five nights?

"Probably both of those things." June scrubbed at her teeth, foam bubbling out of the corners of her mouth. "Did he at least say what he was going to do?"

"He was about to. Then dinner caught on fire." Toby grinned. The memory of the misery etched in Gareth's features had his lips slipping back into a frown. He was going to end up involved after all, wasn't he? "All right, fine. What are the choices she gave him?"

June flipped off the bathroom light and crawled into bed. "What do you know?"

"Not much. She hasn't slept in their room for five days and she gave him two choices, both of which, according to Gareth, suck, and she won't talk to him beyond that. He's really hurting, baby."

She scooted closer, nestling against his chest. "So is she. She told him they either had to talk to an RE or a marriage counselor."

Toby winced. Despite trying to stay out of the details of their life, he had enough information to figure out what was going on. He could see both sides. In Gareth's shoes, Toby would probably be acting the same way. He nuzzled June's hair. "I kind of hope he chooses the counselor."

June sighed. "I hate that I agree with you. It's bad, Toby."

"We'll pray for them. It's all we can do."

7

"Both."

July furrowed her brow and set the stack of dishes she was carrying beside the sink. "Both what?"

"Both options. We can go see an RE, but we're also going to talk with Pastor Brown." Gareth rinsed the stack of plates and loaded them into the dishwasher.

"Why?" July crossed her arms.

"Because on the one hand, you're right that it doesn't hurt to find out what a doctor has to say, provided we're honest with him about all the previous history. No glossing over how close you came to dying."

"And Pastor Brown?"

"Because we're supposed to be a team, partners who talk things out when they disagree. Not adversaries who create situations where someone wins and the other loses." He ran a hand over his face and turned, leaning against the counter. "And if we're really going to explore how medicine can help us have a child, we need to be sure we're parents who are willing and able to stay married for the long haul."

July's eyes widened as a fist closed around her heart. Her voice was strangled. "What do you mean?"

He moistened his lips. "I mean I love you, July. But after how you've treated me this week, I'm not sure I know you anymore. And that scares me. I thought I only had to worry about losing you in childbirth, but this week you've made it clear that I could lose you regardless. I never thought you'd be willing to walk away from me—from us—from the vows we made. Now?" He shrugged. "I'm not so sure."

Her stomach sank through the floor as his words slammed into her heart like bullets. "Gareth."

He shook his head. "I really don't want to hear it. Not right now. I'll call the Pastor. You handle the doctors. Let me know when and where and I'll be there."

As he strode from the room, her knees buckled and she slid to the floor. What had she done?

"I DON'T KNOW what to do." July stared out the window of the sandwich shop. A cold autumn rain pelted against the glass. People scurried across the courtyard, huddled under umbrellas or hunched into their jackets. A tear slipped down her cheek.

June reached across the table and squeezed her hand. "Are you going to make an appointment?"

July shrugged. "What's the point? Gareth'll show up, sure. But his heart's not in it. He doesn't even want to try to make a baby anymore."

"That's not what he said. You gave him two choices, he chose both of them. That doesn't mean anything beyond that he's hurting. You hurt him, Jules. You know that, right?"

Of course she did. Didn't it matter that she was hurting too? She closed her eyes as they filled. She wasn't going to cry. Not right now. Not with an entire afternoon of work ahead of her. "I never intended to pull away for the whole week…but after I stayed in the guest room that first night, it got harder and harder to go back. I knew he'd want to talk about things, hash them out, and I'm so tired of having that same argument. I thought…I thought maybe he'd finally understand that I was serious."

June's eyebrows arched. "Mission accomplished. And, bonus, now you're having a new argument."

July's chest constricted as heat flooded her face. "Whose side are you on?"

"Nobody's. You may not believe me, but it's true. I'm not choosing a side here. You and Gareth have both done things wrong, but right now, I'm not talking to Gareth. And you can't fix the things he's done wrong. Was it okay for him to move to the guest room when you did finally move back into your bedroom? No. Of course not. But Jules…why do you think he did it?"

"I know. And that's the only reason I'm sharing all this dirty laundry with you. I don't know what to do. Even if I had an idea of something to try…I don't trust myself anymore. Look at how well I've done up to now." July pressed the heels of her hands into her eyes. Why hadn't someone invented a time machine yet? If she could just rewind the last week…

June sighed. "At this point I think all you can do is make an appointment with the doctor, go to counseling with Gareth, and pray that God will heal this mess." She pressed her lips together. "And maybe just get up and move beds every time he does. Sleeping apart has to end, even if it means you follow him around the house all night long."

July gave a derisive laugh. "That sounds restful. For both of us."

"Maybe not. But I'm not wrong. It has to stop. Think about it, okay?"

"Yeah, okay."

"Toby and I are praying for you. I don't know what else we can do. But if you think of something, let me know."

July nodded and turned back to the window. The rain had eased a little, though it was still coming down steadily. Her sister said something. The rustling of sandwich wrappers and a chair scraping suggested she was leaving. July didn't turn to look. What else was there to say? Her life was a mess and it was her own fault.

8

"Have a seat, Gareth. Can I get you anything? Some iced tea?"

Gareth smiled at Mary Brown and shook his head. His tongue was glued to the top of his mouth, but tea wasn't likely to fix the problem. His stomach churned. Would tea even stay down? Better not to risk it.

"All right. Paul will be here in just a minute. He's finishing up a little project in our rental unit downstairs. Make yourself comfortable."

Gareth watched Mary disappear down the hall and turned, hands tucked in his pockets. The study just off the foyer was cozy. A chocolate brown leather sofa, complete with subtle indentations in the seats, lined one wall. Bookshelves lined the other walls. The pastor's desk ran parallel to the couch, an office chair tucked in neatly behind it. Its surface was clean, save for a single pile of file folders. Two club chairs were placed in front of the desk, angled to create a conversation area with the couch, though they could easily swivel to face the desk if needed. After a brief hesitation, Gareth settled on one end of the couch and propped an ankle on his knee.

It was a nice space. People probably felt relaxed here, at ease. Maybe he would at some point. He swallowed back bile. Then again, maybe not. All the conversations he'd rehearsed on the drive over fled from his mind as footsteps, followed by muffled voices, echoed down the hall. Gareth cleared his throat. He was right to do this in person. Alone. July might not agree when she found out about it, but then, what had she agreed with lately? His conscience pricked him. Okay, fine. He hadn't been the poster boy for agreeability since Friday either, but wasn't it about time she saw what it was like?

"Gareth." Paul Brown smiled as he closed the study door behind him and extended his hand. "How are you?"

Gareth leaned forward to shake the pastor's hand, returning a weak smile. "Great. I appreciate you seeing me tonight on such short notice."

Paul waved it away as he sat in one of the chairs in front of the desk. "It's no problem. What can I do for you?"

Gareth took a deep breath, willing away the jitterbugs dancing under his skin. "Um. I wanted to talk about," he paused to clear his throat, "this is harder than I thought. July and I...we're having some issues...problems...things are bad."

He dropped his head, fixing his gaze on the tips of his shoes. Silence stretched through the room.

"Can you tell me about it? What's going on?"

There was no censure in Paul's tone. Gareth glanced up. No judgment shone from Paul's eyes, only interest, as if Gareth had said he'd been reading a good book. Some of the weight in his belly lifted.

"It's...kind of a long story."

"I've got all the time you need." Paul shifted in his seat.

Gareth studied him for a moment then nodded and launched into an explanation of the last year, with July's miscarriages, the ectopic, the nightmares that woke him in a cold sweat convinced that July had died, leaving him alone with multiple infants. He finished with their argument last week, her move to the guest room, and her ultimatum.

"So...I finally chose both. But things still aren't right between us. And I don't know if they ever will be."

Paul gave a slow nod. "And your sleeping arrangements?"

Gareth frowned. "She came back into our room on Friday, after I caved. But I was so mad at being manipulated like that...I moved. She didn't follow."

"What are you hoping for?"

What did he mean? What did anyone hope for when they went to marriage counseling? "I don't know how to fix this. I don't know if it can be fixed. I...I'm not even positive I want it fixed. Not if it's going to stay like this. But I feel like we have to try."

GARETH CLENCHED the sheet of paper Pastor Brown had given him and stared at his house. When had he started dreading coming home? He didn't have an answer. But July was in there, probably wondering where he was, and all he could do was wish for something—anything—to keep him from having to go in for another few minutes.

He checked his phone. Nothing. No texts or emails. No new Facebook statuses to catch up on. This was ridiculous. He shoved open the car door and strode to the house.

July sat at the kitchen table, pushing pasta around on her plate. She looked up when he closed the door and offered a tentative smile. "I saved you a plate. It's in the microwave."

"Thanks." He set the paper down on the island and ran a hand through his hair. "I met with Pastor Brown. That's why I'm so late."

She set the fork down with a clatter. "Oh?"

His insides tightened, hardening into knots. "I didn't want

to explain everything over the phone. Or to his secretary." He swallowed. "He wants to meet with us on Saturday. There's homework."

"Okay." July held out her hand.

She couldn't get up and get it? Typical. He grabbed the paper and crossed the room, dropping it in front of her. Her gaze didn't waver and her hand remained outstretched.

"What? It's all there. I figured we could just each do it separately and then compare answers sometime before Saturday."

July shook her head and reached for his hand. "Gareth."

"Yeah?"

She sighed. "I'm sorry. I..."

He lifted his brow.

"I'm just sorry. Will you forgive me?"

Would he? Could he? Pastor Brown's final words echoed in his head—there was nothing he could do for them if Gareth wasn't fully invested. Part of him wanted to scream no. It was convenient that now, having won, she was asking for forgiveness. But...she wasn't one to use those words. Typically they glossed over any arguments, letting "I'm sorry" be the end of the matter. Some of the ice around his heart thawed.

"I'll try."

She closed her eyes, but not before he caught a glimpse of pooling tears. "Thank you."

He waited. Surely there'd be more. Demands that he also apologize, beg her forgiveness, explain that he'd been unreasonable, too? Nothing.

"I'm going to head up."

Her eyes flew open. "You don't want dinner?"

"Not hungry. Thanks though." He offered a tight smile on his way to the stairs.

9

July swallowed the lump in her throat as Gareth clomped upstairs. Tears burned in her eyes. That had been worse than she'd imagined. And she'd imagined it going pretty poorly. Through the hazy blur, she carried her plate to the sink and scraped the cold, uneaten pasta into the disposal. She grabbed the plate she'd fixed for Gareth out of the microwave and added it to the pile before turning on the water and flipping the switch. The greedy gears sucked the food down with a gurgle. Was that where her marriage was headed? She knuckled away the tears, choking back sobs, and turned off the sink. At least he hadn't completely rejected her apology...even if it had looked like he wanted to.

Crossing back to the kitchen table, she scanned the homework from the pastor. It seemed straightforward enough—family history, how they handled conflict and disagreements, why they were there, and what they hoped to achieve. Those last two...July had no answer. She'd thrown it out as an alternative simply because she needed some kind of other choice to offer. Then, he was supposed to give in and they could move on with fertility treatments, because the options made that the clear choice. And that had been incredibly manipulative. She buried her head in her hands. No wonder Gareth was so mad.

Turning off lights as she went, July trudged upstairs. No light shone under the guest room door as she passed it. Maybe he'd migrated back into their room. She hesitated in the doorway, squinting at the bed. Was he in it? Didn't look like it. Tiptoeing, she moved closer. Her shoulders fell. She flipped on the bathroom light and proceeded to get ready for bed. Did she do as June suggested and move into the guest room with him? What if he got up and moved? June said follow him but...how much rejection did you court in situations like this? On the other hand, what was the alternative—letting him think she was okay with the situation? She'd wanted him to fight harder for her to come back to the room last week. She owed it to him —and herself—to fight this.

With a nod at her reflection, she turned out the light, grabbed her pillow, and plodded back down the hall. Holding her breath, she eased open the door and stepped into the dark room. Which side was he on? July aimed for her usual left side. It was still neatly made next to the rumpled lump of Gareth's still form. A smile tugged at her lips. He hadn't transitioned to taking up the whole bed yet. That had to be a good sign. Right?

She dropped the guest pillow on the floor, tucked hers in place, and slipped under the covers.

"Go away, July."

"I thought you were sleeping." She shifted, working a wrinkle of mattress cover smooth so it wouldn't dig into her all night.

"There hasn't been a lot of that going on for a week now. You being here isn't going to help that."

July sighed and rolled over, propping herself on her elbow. In the dim light leaking through the window blinds, she could

Gareth on his back, arms folded across his chest like a corpse, the way he always slept. "I haven't been sleeping very well myself. And I'd venture to say that being in bed with you *will* help both of us. I was wrong to push like I did. If I could rewind the last week—maybe even longer—I would."

"Yeah, well, woulda' shoulda' and all that."

"You said you forgave me."

He sat up. The heat from his scowl made her shrink back. "I did. But I'm still hurt, damn it. Do you even understand what you did?"

July nodded, swallowing. "I actually just pieced it together when I was looking over the pastor's questions. I..." Could she admit it? Should she? "I figured you'd avoid counseling at all costs...it seemed like an easy way to get you to agree to seeing a specialist."

His bark of laughter held no mirth. "That's great. Pretty much proves that you have no respect for me or my opinions, though. So I guess that's good."

"I know it comes across like that. But it's not true. I do respect you—and I love you—but I haven't been willing to consider that your concerns were valid. That was wrong."

"Ya' think?"

"Come on, Gareth. I'm trying...could you meet me half way? Please?"

He sighed and rolled to his side. "We're still going to meet with the pastor."

Of course they were. Her limbs grew heavy and a ball of lead settled in her gut. She didn't want to meet with the pastor...what if, at the end of any attempt at reconciliation, Gareth decided he was better off without her? She forced cheer into her voice. "Of course."

He studied her for several heartbeats then nodded. "Let's go."

"Where?"

"Back to our bed. If nothing else, I've realized why we don't get many repeat visitors. This mattress is horrible."

"So I followed your advice." July glanced around to be sure no one on the nearby benches could hear their conversation. Yesterday's rain had cleared, leaving the ground sodden. But that didn't deter many of the workers in the area from staking claim to their usual lunch haunts. The nip in the air meant winter was on its way. Better to soak up outside breaks while they were still worth taking.

"Oh? How'd it go?" June dropped her fork back into the salad that sat in her lap.

July shrugged. "Pretty well, I guess. We're back in our room now, at least. But he went to see Pastor Brown on his way home from work last night. So...we're off to marriage counseling."

"That might not be such a bad thing. Seems to me I remember reading that couples who take the time to work on keeping their marriages healthy are happier in the long run."

"Yeah? Where'd you read that? Christian Cosmo?" July frowned at the sandwich she'd brought. What had she been thinking? There was mayo on her PB&J. Maybe she'd just get some chips out of the vending machine when she got back to the office.

June snickered. "Something a little more reputable, but I can't remember exactly where. My point was, maybe this is a good thing?"

"I guess. It feels like failure. And worse than that, it's totally my fault. Last night I finally saw a glimmer of Gareth's side of things...we may be back in the same bed, but it hasn't fixed anything."

"I'm sorry."

"Thanks." July pulled a bunch of grapes out of her lunch

bag. "So tell me about the RE appointment. We never did talk about how things went."

June groaned. "Dr. DiCola is a real...piece of work. Let's go with that. He made several pointed barbs about my weight, totally dismissed charting as useful, and cornered us into his treatment plan regardless of what objections we might or might not have."

July grimaced. "You're not going to work with him, are you?"

"I don't know. At this point, I'm going to get the tests he recommended done. After that I guess we'll see. I'm praying about it. I mean, this is the only recommendation we got, so someone, somewhere has had a positive experience with him, right? Maybe he gets easier to deal with once you start treatment."

"I guess that's possible." Though unlikely. But she wouldn't say that. July didn't need to be the one raining on her sister's parade. She did that plenty in her own life. "So what are the tests?"

"Pelvic ultrasound and HSG for me. Semen analysis for Toby. He was going to go do that after work today. Seems a little unfair that he can do his test in a room by himself and I have to be naked in front of at least two technicians."

July chuckled. "I guess. But he has to...you know. That can't be all that easy when you know everyone who saw you go into that room knows what you're doing."

"Okay. I hadn't thought of it that way." June pressed the lid onto her salad container. "Still. I have the ultrasound tomorrow and the HSG Friday. Then I guess we'll know more about where we are. Have you set up a consult yet?"

July shook her head. "I think I'm going to wait until we've met with the pastor a few times. As much as I don't want to go to marriage counseling, I also don't want start on any kind of treatment until I know Gareth's back on board."

June furrowed her brow. "With the baby? Or with your marriage?"

"That's the question, isn't it."

10

"Are you sure you're up for this?"

The side of the bed sank as Toby sat. June drew her knees closer to her chest and nodded.

"I'll be all right in a minute. Just need the ibuprofen to kick in." The muscles in her abdomen contracted and she gasped. They'd said slight cramping. That would teach her to listen to a man describe the side-effects of a procedure he'd never have to undergo.

Toby's face filled with concern. He laid a hand on her shoulder. "I'm sure they'd be okay if we rescheduled."

"No. We've been trying to have Kevin and Lydia over for a while." She groaned and pushed to a sitting position. "Maybe getting up and moving around will help. I'll come down and set the table."

"I got it." Toby stood. "You rest a few more minutes. They won't be here for another..."

The doorbell's chime floated up the stairs.

June gave a wry chuckle. "Second or two?"

"Something like that. All right, lazy bones, I'll go get the door. You come down when you're up to it."

She watched Toby head downstairs. She could do this. Surely the pain would subside soon. She wiggled her legs over the side of the bed and stood, tottering for a moment before she recovered her balance. Like an old woman, June shuffled down the stairs.

"Hey guys. I'm so glad you could come." June smiled and eased into a chair.

"Thanks for having us." Lydia narrowed her eyes. "You okay?"

"I'm good. I had an HSG this afternoon. Everything I read about it said the effects were mostly 'mild cramps' and occasional nausea. Thankfully I haven't felt ill, but it's clear that it was men who wrote about the cramps."

Lydia chuckled. Kevin glanced at Toby, discomfort clear on his face.

"And we won't belabor the point, right babe?" Toby angled his head toward Kevin as he caught June's eye.

"Right. Sorry."

"No biggie. Kevin's a bit of a baby when it comes to medical stuff. Especially if it's medical and female stuff."

"I prefer to think of it as decorum, not squeamishness." Kevin grinned.

"Not to pry, but when will you get the results?" Lydia slipped her hand in Kevin's.

June flicked her gaze to Toby and then Kevin. Both men shrugged. "The tech said everything was clear. I could see the dye go up and through on the monitor while they did the procedure. I won't know all the details on the ultrasound from Tuesday until our next appointment."

Toby cleared his throat. "What's new with you two?"

"Not much, really. We're just chugging along. It's kind of nice." Kevin slung his arm over Lydia's shoulder.

Lydia looked at Kevin. "Actually...I got an interesting phone call this afternoon that I hadn't had a chance to talk to you about."

"That sounds promising. Hang on, I'll get the snacks, and you can tell us all about it." June hurried to the kitchen, wincing at the pain. Maybe she could take another ibuprofen. She pulled the tray of antipasto from the fridge as Toby came in.

"Thought I'd get drinks. Iced tea?"

"Perfect." June leaned back to check that Kevin and Lydia couldn't see them. "Does this seem more awkward than you expected?"

"Maybe a little. But making new friends is always tough. We've been spoiled by having July and Gareth so close all the time."

"Is that what it is?"

He nodded and filled four glasses with tea. "Need any help? I can make a second trip."

"Nah, I got it." June lifted the tray and followed Toby back to the living room. It was good to make new friends, and July and Gareth needed some space to get things figured out...why did it feel like she was going behind their backs? She set the tray on the coffee table. "So, phone call?"

Lydia speared mozzarella wrapped in prosciutto with a toothpick. "I'm off Fridays now, so I was enjoying my leisurely morning around the house, doing a little tidying up." She glared at Kevin when he snorted. "What? I clean. Sometimes. Anyway, the phone rang and I wasn't paying attention, so I just answered it and it was Staci."

Kevin began to cough, his eyes watering. "Brad and Staci? That Staci?"

"That's the one." Lydia looked at June. "You remember, right?"

"Sure. Whatever I hadn't heard through the grapevine, you filled in. And, um, Toby got filled in after that." Heat flooded her cheeks. But everyone knew married couples told each other everything, right?

Lydia laughed. "Figured as much. Not like I could keep my sordid past a secret if I wanted to."

"What did she want?" Deep furrows etched into Kevin's forehead, his frown practically a grimace.

"My thoughts exactly, though I didn't come right out and ask. It took her a while to get around to it, but at the end of the day, it seems she's wised up. She's finally clued into the fact that happy marriages don't happen when neither side is particularly faithful. She was looking for a couple to mentor them and help them work on strengthening their relationship."

June's jaw dropped. "And she called you? For a recommendation, I hope, not because she was looking for you and Kevin to step into that role. Right?"

Lydia shrugged. "Staci's never been the sharpest knife in the drawer."

Kevin shook his head. "It'd be funny if it wasn't so...ridiculous. You said no."

"I was all set to, when my call waiting rang. This time I checked and it was Brad."

"Tell me you ignored it and just hung up. Please." Kevin ruthlessly stabbed a tomato on the tray, squirting juice onto the coffee table.

"Sorry. I figured in for a penny. So I switched over. Brad was calling to warn me that Staci might be calling and just to ignore her and I quote, 'her bizarre delusions.' He went on to tell me that they were just fine—great, in fact—and I that I didn't need to meddle where I wasn't wanted. Then he hung up before I could get a word in."

Toby drained his glass and leaned forward to set it down. "He sounds like a great guy to be married to."

June snickered.

Lydia rubbed her arms. "Yeah, I had a pretty narrow escape

there. Even with all that I went through after that breakup I can look back and see God's protection." She gave Kevin a loving look. "I owe a lot of that to you, I imagine, and all the praying you did."

Kevin kissed her nose. "Knowing you, you relayed all of that to Staci."

"I left out the stuff about bizarre delusions. But I did say that Brad's resistance to the idea was just one of many reasons I didn't think you and I would be a great fit as a mentor couple."

"I can't imagine you'd be telling us this story if there wasn't more to it." June leaned forward.

"She hemmed and hawed for a bit and finally blurted out the little nugget that she's pregnant, Brad insists it's not his baby, she's mostly confident that it is, but can't be one hundred percent sure. They're at each other's throats constantly ever since she got back from visiting her mother and realized that he'd been dating while she was out of town."

Silence covered the room like a thick quilt. June opened her mouth to speak several times, then stopped. What did you say to that?

"That's...wow." Toby clasped his hands behind his head and leaned back in his chair.

"Pretty much." Lydia turned to Kevin. "Say something."

"I'm still struggling to understand how, exactly, we're supposed to be helpful."

"Got me." Lydia reached for another piece of meat-wrapped-cheese.

Kevin scrubbed a hand over his face. "So where'd you leave things?"

"I told her I'd have to talk to you, and that we'd pray about it, but that between Brad's attitude, our history, and just the general murky nature of their situation I wasn't sure how we could help." Lydia sipped her iced tea. "It did occur to me that maybe Maureen, my boss at the Pregnancy Center, and her husband might be a better fit. They've had a solid marriage, but have certainly seen their share of ups and downs. Throw in the weirdness of Staci's pregnancy and, well..."

"That's a great idea. Do you think she'd do it?" The relief in Kevin's voice was practically tangible.

"I'll talk to her on Monday."

A buzz blared from the kitchen. June popped to her feet and headed toward the kitchen. "That's the oven. Why don't you all find a seat at the table? Toby, could you refill drinks?"

Toby set the glasses on the counter before grabbing the tea pitcher out of the fridge. "Feeling better?"

"Lots. Between the story and the extra pill I swallowed when we got the snacks, I just might pull through." June transferred the pan of lasagna from the oven to the stovetop. "After you take those in, could you come back and grab the salad? I think I can get everything else."

JUNE SNUGGLED UP AGAINST TOBY. "I really like them."

"It was fun. I'll admit I didn't think we'd get along as well as we do."

"Why not?" June frowned. Toby wasn't one who normally jumped to conclusions. In fact, it often drove her nuts because he was so open-minded and willing to wait and see.

"Dunno. I guess maybe I listened to too much gossip without looking for the truth underneath the spite. When you and Lydia struck up a friendship last year...I spent a lot of time trying to figure out how to tell you I wasn't on board with that. Then you seemed to drift apart and now...I'm sorry I didn't encourage you to cultivate the friendship and get over whatever hurdle you hit. What was that?"

June sighed. "She got pregnant. Texted me about it all happy just as I was leaving the hospital after visiting July...just a bad set of circumstances. Then she miscarried and I felt awful for not having been as excited as I should have and it just got weird."

"I don't remember her being pregnant. Wouldn't they have said something in class?" Toby dropped his head to rest on hers.

"She miscarried really early. I think I might be the only one she told other than Kevin." She drew in a deep breath and held it for a moment before releasing it.

"What's bugging you?"

"It's stupid."

"Uh-uh. Tell me. It's bothering you and I want to know." He rolled to his side and stared into her eyes. "Let's have it."

"I just...why does God let people get pregnant when it's clear they don't want the child. When the baby is going to cause huge problems? Why does He let children be curses to some and blessings to others? I know the rain falls on the just and the unjust, I get that. But children aren't water...they're so much more. It's not..."

"Fair?" Toby frowned. "I don't know the answer, though I think maybe we have to step back and wonder how much living in a fallen world factors into things. Even then, I don't think we'll ever have the answer. I'm sorry it hurts you."

She kissed him and rolled to her side. He meant to be comforting. Of course he did. Why was it so hard for her to accept? Starting treatment with the RE was supposed to heal these feelings, wasn't it? 'Cause she'd be pregnant soon and it wouldn't matter anymore who was or wasn't able to conceive. Maybe if she told herself that over and over she'd start to believe it. *God...You've got to help me have faith. I don't understand You. And maybe I'm not supposed to, but why would You make me with such a need to understand, a need for some kind of justice, if it was only going to torture me?*

11

July squirmed in the pew. Why was the pastor staring at them? There were so many other people in the congregation, shouldn't he be spreading the joy of his eye contact around? She glanced at Gareth out of the corner of her eye. He didn't seem to notice. Was she just oversensitive? She bit back a sigh. That was probably the case. She and Gareth were having lunch with the Browns, sort of a pre-counseling get-to-know-you thing. She'd much rather run naked through a thorn bush.

"Stop fidgeting," Gareth hissed.

July fought to sit still for the last few minutes of the sermon. She caught only a few of the words, though Gareth was scribbling notes at warp speed. She'd have to sneak a peek later. Maybe go online and listen to the podcast. Maybe not. It wasn't as if God was actually on speaking terms with her right now. She didn't blame Him. Between nearly blowing her relationship with her sister last year and doing as-yet-to-be-determined damage to her marriage...she didn't really deserve His consideration. Though she could sure use it.

"Jules."

She blinked. People were filing out of the pews to the soft piano music of the postlude. "Sorry."

Gareth sat back down. "What's going on?"

How did he not get this? She reached down to grab her purse. "I'm fine. Let's go, we don't want to be late."

He curled his fingers around her forearm. "There's no rush. The pastor's up there still chatting with people. Talk to me."

"Really? Here?" She lowered her voice to a fierce whisper. "Okay. I don't want to do this. I'm only doing it because you've made it clear that the only possible way you're going to think about forgiving me is if we do. But it's hard to live with an axe over your neck, not knowing if you're going to decide you're still in this marriage."

Gareth's laugh was short and mirthless. "That fact that you can say that and mean it tells me we need this more than I realized. Obviously we're not communicating very well. I told you I forgave you."

"Talk is cheap, Gar. You said it, that's true. But you haven't acted like it. So it sure seems like you just said empty words out of some sense of obligation." She cleared her throat and offered an overly bright smile to the older woman staring at them from three pews away.

His Adam's apple bobbed as he swallowed. "Maybe that's fair. I..."

She held up a hand. "Later, okay. We've already given that woman enough gossip to last her at least a week. She'll be talking about that poor young couple who couldn't even wait to get out of the sanctuary before they started in on each other. I love you. I miss feeling like you love me back. Come on, Mrs. Brown is up there now, too. We might as well go get this over with."

≈

"So, July, why don't you tell us why you think we're here. I've spoken to Gareth already and have his side, but I always like to get a feel for everyone's thoughts before going any further." Paul Brown folded the wrapper to his sub into a neat square and tucked it under the takeout cup of soda in front of him.

July fought the urge to sigh and looked around the pastor's dining room instead. It was a surprisingly modest space in line with the rest of their home. Cozy. Comfortable. It must have been nice to grow up here, though being a pastor's daughter wasn't something she'd ever envied. Who wanted to live in a fishbowl like that?

"We're having communication problems. Over the last year, the issue of children has pushed us in opposite directions and whenever the subject comes up. We talk at or around each other, but never *to* one another. I got fed up and made an ultimatum that I didn't really mean. But that did even more damage to our relationship. And now we're here because Gareth called my bluff and has made it clear that regardless of my thoughts on the matter, if we can't fix the communication problem to his satisfaction he's ready to walk away."

"I never said I was ready to walk away. Don't put words in my mouth." Gareth glared across the table at July.

Mary's voice was quiet, but firm. "You may not have said the words, but it's clear that July felt that's what you meant. Take a minute and think back through what you've said, especially in anger. Did you say anything she might have misconstrued?"

Gareth pursed his lips. "Maybe."

The words were seared in her mind. Should she tell him? July glanced at Mrs. Brown who gave a slight shake of her head.

"That's actually not too far off from what Gareth said." Paul looked at Gareth. "And, Gareth, you said a few things to me that suggested you weren't completely committed to staying. So whether you consciously admit it or not, your mind has gone there."

Gareth opened his mouth, his face burning a bright red. His jaw snapped shut with an audible click.

What was he thinking? From his clenched jaw, she could tell he was fighting his temper. She didn't want everyone to gang up on him—even if it might convince him she wasn't the only one at fault here.

"Okay. I can think of a few things I said, but I'm not...I didn't mean them." Gareth sighed. "So maybe...I'm sorry, Jules. I shouldn't have let you think I wasn't committed to our marriage. I am. But I also think we need help. This is just another example."

She gave a slight nod. Maybe they both needed to work on not saying things for effect or going to extremes. Though since she was more likely to do it, she wasn't going to mention that aloud.

Paul smiled. "In that case, I think we have a good place to start. One of the major things we're going to work on is communication. It's probably all stuff you know, but it's easy to forget in the heat of the moment. So, since you said the root of the problem stems from starting a family, the first thing I want you each to do is write down your argument. Don't refute the arguments you've been throwing at one another, just state your case. Try to be objective as possible, and don't be afraid to do several drafts."

"Then what?" July didn't mind writing it down, but they'd been through this so many times. Was having it on paper really supposed to change anything?

"We'll talk about it next time we get together. But I also want you to think about why you got married in the first place. What are you hoping marriage is going to do for you?" Paul tapped his fingers together.

July frowned. "What do you mean?"

Mary cleared her throat. "One of the things we find so often, particularly with younger couples, is that, in their minds, marriage was supposed to be a vehicle for future happiness. When you're in that first blush of love—you know, when the sun shines brighter, the birds chirp more clearly—it's easy to think marriage is only going to intensify that and that every day you're together it's just going to get better. But it's just not the case."

The corners of July's mouth twitched. Mary had that right. The shine had rubbed off after about a year.

Gareth sipped his soda. "We're both from parents who are still together. I think we know marriage takes work."

"Work is part of it, true." Mary's gaze traveled between July and Gareth. "But you have to be working at the right thing. It's not about you. It's not even about your spouse."

"Then what is it about?" July clenched her hands into fists in her lap fighting to keep the scorn out of her voice. Of course Gareth wasn't there to make her happy, that was her own responsibility. But the main point of their pre-marital counseling was that they were both to focus on the other and that was how their marriage would be strong. Now Mary was saying they had it all wrong?

Paul reached over and twined his fingers with Mary's. "Marriage is about refining you into the image of Christ. Just like everything else in our spiritual walk. And in marriage, God uses your spouse to reveal things about you that He wants to work on—whether or not your spouse ever changes."

"But if I'm learning how to be patient with someone who dismisses my feelings out of hand, shouldn't she be learning to be more considerate of those feelings?" Gareth's gaze slid to July.

Oh sure, she was the dismissive one. July narrowed her eyes at him and opened her mouth to speak.

Paul shook his head. "Of course, but it's not up to you to be her Holy Spirit. If you're feeling like God is asking you to work on patience, then that's where your focus needs to lie. On your own spiritual development. As you both seek God's kingdom first in your own life, the rest—in this case a happier marriage included—is going to follow."

July swallowed, the pastor's words rolled around in her mind. They made sense. If she was honest, over the last year things had definitely shifted in her spiritual life. Had she become so focused on having a baby that she'd abandoned her relationship with God? When was the last time she'd done a Bible study or prayed without an underlying ulterior motive of convincing God to give them a baby?

Gareth ran a hand through his hair. "All right...I can see that. I don't like it, but I see it."

Mary chuckled. "I don't think anyone likes it when they first start to realize that the ideal of marriage our culture promotes is off balance. But as Christians it's so important that we discover God's purpose for marriage—not just our marriage, but in general—is to draw us nearer to Himself."

"So, that's the second part of your homework." Paul smiled. "Write down what you've been expecting of your marriage and your spouse. Then ask if those things are going to contribute to your spiritual growth or if they're based on some Hollywood fairytale fabrication. Finally, ask God to show you His plan for your relationship and how He's using this season of your marriage to help you grow in Him."

"Okay." July studied her hands. It was a tall order...would she be able to handle the results?

Paul looked at Mary. "What about doing lunch again next Sunday? We'll keep things somewhat informal, friendlier. Bring your write-ups with you. In the meantime, try to focus on taking a breath before you argue. And remember to say 'I feel' and 'it seems to me' rather than 'you ought to', particularly when you're disagreeing. And pray about the irritations you see in each other, ask God to show you what *you* should change in response."

"Lunch sounds great. We don't have any family obligations for a while, and food always makes things feel less threatening." Mary gave a serene smile. "Plus...don't neglect your intimacy. I realize things have been tense, but you need that time together. It'll reassure each of you that things will get better, that the other loves you."

Heat flooded July's face. No matter how delicate Mary had been, talking about her sex life with the pastor and his wife wasn't on July's list of things to do. Ever.

Gareth cleared his throat. "Yeah. Um. Okay."

~

JULY CRAWLED into bed and rolled to face Gareth. "I'm sorry. This whole mess...I feel like it's my fault."

Gareth shook his head and flipped to face her. "Not entirely. We've both made some mistakes lately. But we can fix it. Right?"

"I hope so. I want to. I wish we could just go back to before all this happened."

"Maybe we'll end up stronger for going through it. That's what everyone says, right?"

"I've never really appreciated those people." She moistened her lips. "Do you want...should we..."

A gleam lit in Gareth's eyes and he nodded. "Yeah."

12

"Okay, let's see what we've got here." Dr. DiCola flipped open a folder and paged through several sheets affixed to a brad at the top of the left side. "HSG looks good. Ultrasound...not terrible. You've got a fairly classic case of PCOS—had your doctor done anything to treat that?"

June shook her head, wishing Toby had been able to come. "She was only comfortable with trying Clomid or putting me on the pill for symptom control. Since that didn't make any sense when we want to start a family, I've just been trying to lose the weight. Or at least keep it from piling on."

He gave a brief nod. "We'll prescribe Metformin along with the rest then." He flipped a few more pages and scribbled a notation. "I think the lowest dose of the follicle stimulation should be a good place to start. No reason it shouldn't work. So we just need to wait for your cycle to start. Call us on day one and we'll get your protocol set up. You'll want to have these prescriptions filled. Start the Metformin right away, the rest just keep on hand until we get started. Any questions?"

Hundreds of them raced through her brain. What was Metformin? What were the side effects? Was it okay to take while pregnant or just before hand? But if she'd learned anything at the first appointment, it was that he didn't actually mean it when he asked for questions. So June pushed her lips into a smile.

"No. I don't think so."

"Great." He ripped several sheets off a prescription pad and offered them to her. "Call the desk on day one of your cycle. Until then, try not to worry."

Right. She stood, clutching the prescriptions. At least there hadn't been anything appreciably wrong. Having the ultrasound confirm PCOS was a good thing, right? She'd do more research on the rest of the stuff when she got home. Dr. DiCola might not want informed and educated patients, but she wasn't going to simply sit by and trust him without knowing what she was putting into her body and why.

She stopped at the front desk to ask for a copy of her test results. That'd give her more information to look up online.

"Hey, where were you on Sunday? We looked for you." June dropped onto the bench next to her sister.

"Went to the late service so we could have lunch with the pastor and his wife." July unzipped her insulated lunch bag. "Before you ask, it went okay, but no, I don't want to talk about it."

June pursed her lips and watched her sister for a moment, questions burning the tip of her tongue. It wasn't her business. If her sister didn't want to talk about it, it was fine. It was. She gave a short nod. "All right. How's work?"

"Fine. I got the last batch of clients with tax extensions filed this morning. So that's a relief. Now I'm back to only having to deal with the day-to-day business of my corporate clients. And frankly, that's not all that challenging. It's good to have a break on the horizon. What about you?"

"Work's fine. After all the issues last year, I keep looking for the other shoe to drop, but so far so good. I do see Paula lurking around on our floor periodically. That woman...maybe she has actual business to attend to, but I suspect she's hoping to find some dirt somewhere. The problem, of course, is that there isn't any." June sighed and unwrapped the protein bar she'd brought for lunch. "I just hope the people on my team like me well enough to tell me if they hear anything. I think they do...but I never knew Anthony had a problem with me until it blew up in my face."

July nodded. "How did all the tests go last week?"

"Nothing out of the ordinary, really. Tubes are clear, the ultrasound showed PCOS. But Dr. DiCola seemed pretty certain his typical regimen would work." June chewed a bite of the peanuty-bar. "I can't help being a little, I don't know, annoyed? Frustrated? He's just shoehorning us into his treatment plan without seeming to care what we want."

"Have you mentioned that to him?"

June gave a bark of laughter. "I told you about when I tried to ask questions at our first visit. There's no way I'm going to question him again. It's very clear—you work with him his way or you find someone else. At this point I'm going to try and trust that he knows what he's doing. The stats on their website certainly indicate that, so..."

"That's not like you. You're just going to blindly follow his plan?"

"Not blindly. I've got a stack of things I'm going to research when I get home. But unless something major turns up...we'll see how it goes."

"When will you start?"

"Hopefully soon." There was no need to get into the fact

that *irregular* was too loose a word for what her cycles had become over the last year. If it took too long, she'd call Dr. Strong about jump starting things. But until then, she was going to trust that things would work out. What other choice was there?

13

July tossed her jacket over the back of a dining room chair on her way to the sofa. What a day it had been. There was no reason for the general haze of blue that seemed to shroud everything. And yet, there it was. Gareth had called several times during the day to let her know he loved her and check on how she was. She hadn't realized he'd stopped doing that until he started doing it again. She stretched out on the couch, eyes drifting shut. When had that happened? Over the summer, most likely. That was when everything had fallen apart. What other signals had she missed?

"You're in my spot."

July cracked open an eye. Had she fallen asleep? Gareth hovered, his nose practically touching hers, a grin flirting with the corners of his mouth.

"I didn't see your name on it." She sat up and made room for him.

"How was your day?" Gareth lifted her legs and sat, draping her feet over his lap. He began to knead the arch of one foot.

"Ahh. Better now. Though it wasn't bad, really. Had lunch with June, worked on client stuff. You know, same old."

"What's new with June and Toby? We didn't get to see them this weekend. I'm sorry." He switched to the other foot.

"Mmm. Not much, actually. She finished all the tests the RE wanted her to do. Toby did his. Everything looks good, basically, so they'll start with ovulation induction drugs soon. I hope it works. It's so...unfair, I guess, that she hasn't at least gotten pregnant. Even though I miscarried, I feel guilty, you know?"

Gareth frowned. "Not really. Isn't it better not to conceive than to start a baby and lose it?"

July shrugged. "I don't know. Maybe neither one is better—they just suck differently."

Gareth chuckled. His fingers stilled. "Have you made an appointment for us yet?"

She shook her head. "I thought, given the circumstances, that it was better to wait."

"Make the appointment, babe. You weren't wrong when you said there was no harm in seeing what they had to say. I...overreacted. I don't want to lose you, that hasn't changed. But I don't want to push you away, either."

She sighed. It was a nice sentiment, but was there any point? Sure, things seemed to be going well right now, but how quickly would that change? But what if it didn't change and she made things bad again by not taking him at his word?

"Let's wait a little while, okay?"

Gareth gave her foot a squeeze. "Whenever you're ready, make the appointment." He caught and held her gaze. "I'm on board, Jules. For everything."

She offered a faint smile. "Thanks."

"Why don't we order in, maybe put on a movie?"

JULY STARED AT THE PHONE. Last night, Gareth had been so sincere. Should she call and set up an appointment? It was what she wanted, wasn't it? It had been. Now...she wanted things back the way they were. Back before the need to tiptoe around each other. Did he feel it too?

She picked up the handset and dialed.

"Hello?"

"Hi...Mrs. Brown? It's July?"

"Oh, July, how lovely of you to call. Please call me Mary, would you?"

"Sure. Of course. Thank you."

Mary chuckled. "How are you?"

"I don't know, actually. I was wondering—well, do you have a few minutes?"

"Of course."

July blew out a breath. Where did she start? "I...so much of our argument circled around starting a family and now Gareth says that he's on board with seeing a specialist to at least have an evaluation."

"That's wonderful."

"Is it? How do I know he's not just doing it to humor me? I mean, for so long he fought it, wouldn't even consider it long enough for me to explain why I felt like I needed to know, one way or another, if they could help us. Now, *boom*, he's on board?"

"Mmm. Sounds like you're having trouble trusting his word."

"Exactly. How do I know that it's not going to come back and bite me later?" Why was she so worried about that? She should be able to get past this.

"You don't. Not really." There was a smile evident in Mary's voice. "I know that's not the comfort you were hoping for, but at the end of the day, marriage is built on trust. Right now, you and Gareth are struggling with that. But your trust hasn't been broken, just bruised. It might be a deep bruise, but it's going to fade, and there shouldn't be any residual damage."

"When? I want things back the way they used to be."

"Things will never be exactly the way they used to be, and that's part of life. Every experience changes us, shapes us. But as far as your default response being to trust? How long that takes is totally dependent on you. The sooner you start practicing it, even when it's hard, the sooner it'll become second nature again."

"So I have to trust in order to be able to trust again?" That figured. Yet another entry in the chicken and egg dilemma that plagued the world. Right up there with the other delightful entries like: you have to have experience to get a job where you can gain experience and you have to have money to save money.

"Unfortunately, yes. But you can work on little things—you don't have to jump into the big things right away."

"Is seeing a specialist a big thing or a little thing?"

"That's something you have to decide. But if you decide it's big, then find something small that you can do today."

"Okay. Thanks."

"You're welcome. Anytime."

July set the phone down and leaned back in her office chair. That wasn't the most helpful phone conversation she'd ever had. Though it had given her food for thought. Just not the answers she'd wanted. Why couldn't one single thing in life be cut and dry with clear instructions that guaranteed positive outcomes?

Trust. All right. Fine. She'd trust. Taking a deep breath she reached for the phone again.

14

"Hey. What are you two doing here?" June crossed the waiting room and sat facing July and Gareth.

July's shoulders fell. Perfect. "Just an initial consult. Probably end up with the same test prescriptions you had. What about you?"

"I wanted to pick up copies of our test results so I had all the actual information instead of just 'it all looks fine.' That's good and everything, but I don't know how to quantify 'fine.'"

Gareth grinned. "You're such an engineer."

"Yes. Yes I am. Toby is too, if that helps? So at least we can be analytical and annoying together?"

"That's not what I meant." Gareth frowned.

"Gotcha. I know that. Well, good luck with your consult. Hopefully you'll get Dr. Jekyll instead of Mr. Hyde. Though I haven't seen any evidence that Jekyll exists." June stood. "Call me and let me know how it goes, 'k? And I'll be starting injections tomorrow, so if you think about it, you could pray for me."

July nodded. "Will do."

"What's the big deal with injections? She looked ready to

faint." Gareth watched his sister-in-law wind through the chairs in the waiting room to the exit.

"June has a long-standing phobia of needles. She's got to be pretty desperate if she's going to not only have shots, but give them to herself. Wonder why Toby isn't doing it for her."

"I'd have a hard time giving you shots, and I've got a medical degree. I imagine Toby offered though. As will I, if the time comes." He smiled.

July returned the smile, but her heart wasn't in it. They weren't going to need that kind of intervention, were they? She could get pregnant. Just couldn't manage to stay that way. Surely that would alter the prescribed manner of treatment. July suppressed a shudder. June's needle phobia was nothing compared to her own.

"That's us. You ready?" Gareth stood, offering her a hand.

She took it. Was she ready? No. But this was the next logical step, so they'd take it.

"HE WASN'T VERY OPTIMISTIC, was he?" July scooted toward the wall to make more room in the booth for Gareth.

"Not so much. But maybe the tests will help him see what's going on, why you keep miscarrying."

"I guess. I'd just hoped we'd leave with an answer. Something clear that explained everything." July shrugged. "There's never an easy answer, I know that. But I keep hoping for one all the same."

"Let's not worry about it until we've gotten the tests out of the way. If he's still concerned at that point, then..."

"Hey!" June rushed across the crowded restaurant. Toby and another couple trailing in her wake. "We bumped into Kevin and Lydia out front. Can they join us?"

July looked at the booth. It would seat six if they didn't

mind being cozy. Maybe having another couple there would keep the conversation off of marriage counseling and infertility. After the less-than-positive experience at the doctor this afternoon, she could use a break.

"Sure. Why not. We'll squeeze." July scooted until her leg touched the booth wall and tugged Gareth closer. "Plenty of room."

June gestured for Kevin and Lydia to slide in the other side of the booth. "Why don't you two slide in there, and we'll see which side has more room. Toby gets the smaller side since he takes up less space these days."

"So what'd the doctor say?" June leaned around Gareth to peer at July.

So much for not talking about it. But she wasn't going into details. She waved a dismissive hand. "Have to wait and see what the tests show."

Gareth opened his mouth. July kicked him. He frowned and cleared his throat, glancing across the table at Kevin and Lydia. "How's the small group going?"

"Pretty well. We'll be starting a new study in another two, maybe three weeks if you two want to come back and join us again." Kevin reached for the water glass the server was passing down.

"Um. Probably not going to happen any time soon. It's not anything personal. Just..." Gareth glanced at July.

July's head flopped against the back of the booth. Was she ever going to catch a break? "Maybe you already know...we're seeing Lydia's folks for counseling on Sundays at lunch for a little while. Working out some kinks in how we communicate."

"Aha. You're the mysterious reason we can't have lunch after church anymore." Lydia grinned. "Which is totally fine, by the way. And hey, if anyone can help you figure out communication issues, it's my folks. They're great."

"I'll second that. Paul helped me a lot when I was going

through some stuff before Lydia and I got together. Would it be all right if we prayed for you?" Kevin unrolled the napkin containing his silverware.

"Prayer is always good. But maybe just you two? Don't mention it to the class or anything." July pulled her lower lip between her teeth.

"Of course not." Lydia stuck a straw in her water and looked at June. "Did you fill them in on the Staci and Brad thing?"

June shook her head. "I wasn't sure if that would be okay or not. I'm trying to be better about that."

Lydia laughed. "I don't mind. Maybe from a gossip standpoint you're more virtuous than me though. But that's not going to stop me." She paused to take a sip of water then summarized the conversation she'd had with Staci the week before. "So on Monday I asked Maureen about her availability. She agreed to chat with them, and see what, if anything she could offer but she asked me to sit in since I knew them."

"Doesn't she know the history there?" Kevin dunked a chip into some salsa.

"I told her. Didn't get her to budge. So..." Lydia trailed off as the server arrived to take their orders then disappeared again. "Anyway, Wednesday, Brad and Staci came in to the pregnancy center and sit down in Maureen's office and when the whole tale was finally out in the open, I found myself feeling a little sorry for Staci."

July frowned. How did you get to the point you could feel sorry for someone who'd caused that much trouble in your life? "Wow."

"Yeah, pretty much. I certainly never expected that to happen. Brad, well, he's still a class A jerk. He even hit on Maureen. I thought she might just come out from behind the desk and hit him. Long story short, Brad isn't really interested in any kind of relationship development—that's why they aren't seeing my parents for counseling anymore. He's completely satisfied with their, as he termed it, *arrangement*. He says Staci was on board when they got together and he's always been clear about the fact that there was nothing exclusive about the two of them."

"What'd Staci say to that?" July reached for the chips, putting a handful on the table in front of her to cut down on how much reaching she had to do.

"She admitted it was true, but she said having a baby made her realize things needed to change. At least a little. Brad then went on a rampage about how she couldn't prove the baby was his and they'd just have to wait and see how that turned out before he was even willing to consider it."

Gareth leaned forward, propping his elbows on the table. "They can do paternity testing during pregnancy. Either as part of a CVS or an amnio."

Lydia chuckled. "Almost word-for-word what Maureen said. I was actually a little surprised by that as neither procedure is one we usually recommend. They're very invasive and pose risks to the baby. But I guess in this instance maybe the potential for good outweighs that. Either way, Staci was going to talk to her doctor about it."

July leaned back to make room for her food as the server appeared with an overloaded tray balanced on her shoulder. "What did Brad say about that?"

"He's as on board as he's likely to get, I think. But until that, the final takeaway is Staci needs a friend and Maureen volunteered me for the job...and I'm drafting June, and July you too if you're willing, to be in on it. I can't fathom trying to do anything with her without some external support."

June blinked.

July's jaw dropped. Didn't the woman have any other friends?

"What about Laura? And what's-her-name? The lawyer?" June waved her arms, nearly knocking over the drinks on that side of the table.

"Oh, I'm going to try and rope them into it too, have no fear. But..."

Kevin shook his head. "They're going to plead new baby, aren't they? That's the only excuse we get with either couple lately. Like somehow because we don't happen to have a new baby we're not willing to hang out with people who do. And frankly it's getting annoying. We've been friends with them long enough—especially Matt and Laura—they should understand the fact that they have kids and we don't isn't a big deal."

"Wow. A little repressed anger there, Kev?" Lydia bumped his shoulder with hers.

July looked across at her sister. If she and Gareth had a baby, would June and Toby no longer be available? No...that was ridiculous. "Well, with that ringing endorsement for why my presence is desired, how can I say no?"

June laughed. "I don't think it was meant as back-handed as it came out."

"No, of course it wasn't." Lydia tapped her fork against her plate. "So, next Friday don't make plans. We're doing something with Staci. What, exactly, I don't know yet. But we'll figure something out."

"Might I suggest a movie? That way all you have to do is sit next to each other and not interact." Toby eyed June's plate before reaching across and stealing an olive.

"Hey." June stabbed at his hand with her fork. "Though the movie's not a bad idea."

"Already had that thought...and got it vetoed by Maureen. She specifically said it had to be something interactive. So if you have any ideas, make sure you text me. I'm trying to convince myself this isn't going to be a nightmare."

Kevin snickered. "How's that working?"

Lydia stuck out her tongue.

"So, I guess that means you're free next Friday, Kevin." Gareth looked at Toby. "Want to see if we can find a fourth and break out the poker chips?"

15

Toby opened the door to find Kevin and two other guys chatting on the front step. "Hey. Come on in."

"I brought two more, if that's all right?" Kevin grinned and clapped Toby on the shoulder. "You know Phil from small group, right? And this is his friend Grant."

"I think we've met, yes." Toby shook Phil's hand, then Grant's. "Glad you could join us. Gareth's setting up the table, straight in, turn left."

He closed the door and watched as they tromped into the dining room. He should follow, but this wasn't anywhere in his top ten things he wanted to be doing tonight. Having June out of the house wasn't on that list either. Not that he minded her going out with the girls, though this particular outing didn't rank high on his list of things she should be involved in. Still, she'd wanted to go and try to help Lydia so they'd have a quiet night tomorrow. He'd deal with having people in the house after a long, stressful week. And he'd try not to think about how much he'd rather be playing a computer game.

"Who needs a drink? We have water, various soda, all diet

unfortunately, since June does the shopping, and some iced tea that I made so it has real sugar in it."

When Toby had returned with the drinks, Gareth tapped the deck of cards on the table and began shuffling. "Okay, the game is Texas Hold 'Em. Because that's the only one I know how to play. Everyone's in for five bucks to keep it honest and more fun. And hey, with five of us playing, that's actually a decent amount of money in the pot. July and I will enjoy our night out courtesy of you fine folks."

Phil scoffed and looked at Grant. "Cocky, isn't he?"

Grant shook his head. "Maybe he has the skills to back it up. Does he know we used to play every week?"

Gareth's head swiveled to Kevin, his eyes narrowing. "You brought card sharks?"

Kevin shrugged. "I brought Phil, he brought Grant. What they did with their time in their mis-spent bachelor-hood is not my problem."

"Hey. Some of us there aren't bachelors." Grant wiggled his fingers at Gareth. "Deal the cards, man."

Phil looked at Grant. "You still play on Fridays?"

Grant caught his cards as they slid across the table. "It's more like every-other-week now that most of the guys have gotten married again. But it's still fun. If you can pry yourself away from Allison and the baby, you should join us sometime."

"I might just do that." Phil smirked. "I can always use some extra cash."

"Ha. Don't listen to the lawyer." Kevin picked up his cards and frowned.

"Nice poker face, Kev." Toby laughed and picked up his own cards. Not a bad hand. A quick glance around the table had him raising the bet.

"So what's new with you and June, Toby? We haven't seen much of you at church." Phil scratched his temple before tossing another chip into the center.

How much was he allowed to say? Toby imagined Kevin knew everything because of Lydia. Gareth, too. He bit back a sigh. She'd have to get over it if she was annoyed. "We're seeing a fertility specialist. So the baby boom in the class has been a bit of a challenge—for both of us, though I think June's taking it the hardest. Especially once she realized the babies were going to actually be *in* the class. I think she expected it to get easier once all the pregnant stomachs went away. Why *are* the babies in the class? Isn't that why the church has a nursery?"

Phil held up his hands. "Don't look at me. I asked the same question when Allison started up the stairs with the baby carrier. She didn't explain the look she gave me, but I didn't push or ask again because I'm enjoying being married this time around and I'd like to stay that way." The guys all snickered. "I'm sorry it's hard though."

Toby shrugged. "Thanks. Anyway, that's really the only big thing going on."

Gareth dealt the last card into the river. "How's the treatment going? July and I had a consult this afternoon—lots of tests lined up. Be nice to know what we're in for with the next step."

"Eh. So far I haven't had to do anything more than watch her give herself shots. And stay out of her way—the hormones in those drugs are already making her crazy. We've got at least another week of it, too. Hopefully it'll work the first time. I really don't want to have to deal with months and months of raging hormones."

"Dude. If it works, you're going to have at least nine more months of raging hormones. Allison was a whole different person—and I'm not exaggerating, well not much anyway." Phil threw his cards down on the table. "I fold."

"Great." Toby shook his head and tossed a few more chips on the growing pile in the middle of the table. At least the every-other-day ultrasound appointments would stop once she got pregnant. He suspected she'd be easier to deal with if she was back to getting consistent sleep instead of having to keep waking up early to get to the doctor's office before seven in the morning.

Gareth flipped the last card onto the table. "All right, ladies. Let's see 'em."

Laughing, Kevin, Toby, and Grant dropped their hands face up. Toby shot a fist in the air and flexed his bicep. "Yes." He raked the chips toward his spot at the table. "I don't think it's you and July who'll be dining on the winnings, Gar."

"Yeah, yeah." Gareth stacked the cards and dropped them in front of Toby. "Your deal."

Toby split the cards into two stacks and began to shuffle, then deal. "So, Grant. Tell us a little about yourself."

TOBY SHUT the door and stuffed his hands in his pockets as he ambled back into the dining room. "That went well, I think."

Gareth didn't look up from sorting and stacking the chips back into his case. "Yep. Grant seems nice."

"He does." Toby frowned as he collected cups, plates, and pizza boxes. "Are you and July okay?"

"I don't know." Gareth sighed and scrubbed a hand over his face. "I want to say yes, but things are different. I'm guessing they're not going to ever go back to the way they were. Some of that's not bad, we're definitely communicating better now. But it's like the innocence is gone. Does that make sense?"

Toby nodded. Hadn't the same thing happened between him and June? Sure, they weren't in counseling, but maybe they should be. For now they were okay, but it was like walking through a jungle you knew was inhabited with enemies. You never knew when you were going to take a step and fall into a pit of stakes. Or snakes. Or worse.

"I know I convinced July to go ahead and make the appointment for the specialist, but dude, after talking to the man today...he makes it sound like we're guaranteed a baby in ten months. I'm not there anymore." Gareth's shoulders sagged. "But I can't go back on it now. So what do I do?"

"Like I have any answers here." Toby gave a short laugh. "All you can do is pray for discernment. And maybe tell July how you feel."

Gareth scoffed. "That'd go over well. She was all set to wait for a while on this, I pushed her back into it."

"So just tell her you're nervous. She probably is too. Maybe it'll help to know you're in the same place?" Toby carried the stack of dishes and trash into the kitchen. He shouldn't be giving advice, he barely understood his own wife now that they were in the middle of this mess.

Gareth leaned in the doorway between the dining room and kitchen. "I'm gonna run. I imagine the girls'll be back before much longer. I'd like to have a few minutes to unwind before I get an earful about their night."

Toby laughed and dried his hands. "Sounds good."

"YOU'RE STILL UP?" June dropped her purse on the kitchen table and tapped the top of Toby's book.

"I got caught up." He tugged the business card from the back of the book and stuck it in as a bookmark. "How was your evening?"

"Fun. Though Staci never showed. Lydia called her a few times, never got more than really loud music on the other end of the phone. We figure she went out partying. But the three of us had a good time. I didn't expect Lydia and July to get along, honestly, but they've hit it off." June pulled out the chair next to him and sat. "What about you?"

"It was good. Kevin brought Phil—you remember him and Allison from small group? And I guess Phil brought his friend Grant, who seems pretty cool."

"Mm. I remember Phil, but not Grant. What's his wife's name?"

"He's not in the small group. I don't think he's still married. He mentioned a wife, obliquely, but the vibe was that she's not in the picture anymore."

"Divorced?"

Toby shook his head. "I got the feeling she'd passed away. I didn't want to pry and it seemed like old news to everyone else. On the plus side, you and I have our next dinner out subsidized."

"Way to go." She patted his knee. "Gareth say anything about how things were going with July?"

"Not really. He's nervous about seeing the RE—I told him that meant he wasn't stupid. Otherwise?" Toby shrugged.

"July was quiet, too. She did say their second lunch with the Browns went well...it's hard though. I want to respect their privacy, but at the same time..."

"I know." He leaned forward to kiss her. "They'll share what they're comfortable with, when they're comfortable doing it. Until then, we keep praying."

"You're right. Still." Tears welled in June's eyes and she blinked them furiously. "I just want our baby to have a solid family. And that includes her aunt and uncle."

Toby sighed. The tears were always right at the surface now that June was a week into the medication. It was the worst part so far. He'd take a screaming match any day over tears. "They're going to be okay...how are you feeling?"

June wiped her eyes and blew out a breath. "Fine. These hormones are nuts though, I'm sorry."

"It's all right. You're sure?"

"Why don't you come upstairs and I'll show you?"

16

"How are things going?" Paul Brown folded his hands on the dining room table and looked at Gareth and July.

July glanced at Gareth. He nodded at her. All right, she'd go first.

"Good, I think." Out of the corner of her eye she caught Gareth nodding and smiled. "We did go see the specialist. I'm... nervous, I guess, about that. But the idea of having answers is better than not knowing."

"You're nervous too?" Gareth's eyes grew wide.

"Yeah. Why wouldn't I be?"

Gareth shrugged. "You just seemed so sure that it was the right thing...I figured I was the only one with reservations."

Mary Brown chuckled. "It does seem like you're communicating better. Two weeks ago, I can't imagine this conversation being so pleasant."

July winced. "Probably not."

"Gareth, do you have anything to add?" Paul lifted his brows.

"Not really. I agree that we're doing better. Knowing that

we're both nervous helps, too." Gareth pursed his lips. "A new perspective hasn't hurt, either. I think we've both been working to see our marriage as a way for God to refine us individually, and as a couple, instead of a way for us to be individually fulfilled. I know for me, at least, that way of thinking has made it easier to step back and take a deep breath when I'm frustrated. And that cuts down on the arguing."

July chuckled. "I've been taking that step back as well. And really working on saying things right—not just the way they first occur to me. Seems like that's an area God's really been working on me, my tendency to just blurt out my thoughts without considering how that's going to come across to someone else. For me, at least, there haven't been nearly as many instances where I've found myself getting frustrated."

"They're definitely diminishing." Gareth grinned and reached for her hand.

"Phew." July drew her hand across her forehead as if wiping away sweat.

Mary laughed. "That's lovely to hear. And it's been lovely to see the two of you working so hard on this. So many couples come to us for help without wanting to do the work—particularly when we start pointing out that we're not here to fix the other person but to let God change us into who He wants us to be."

"I'll admit, when we first started I was hoping you'd tell her I was right." Gareth offered a sheepish shrug.

July squeezed his hand. "So was I. Well, not that they'd say you were right, but you know what I mean. And now that things are so much smoother between us, I'll go ahead and schedule the tests the specialist ordered. I've been putting them off, not knowing if it was really the right thing."

"Why wouldn't it have been the right thing?" Mary folded her hands in front of her.

"I guess because I'm trying not to only focus on what I want and really take into consideration Gareth's side of things. If he wasn't ready, really ready, I didn't want us to start down a path that he was against."

"Babe." Gareth pursed his lips. "I told you I was on board."

July shrugged. "I know. And second guessing is on my list of things I'm working on."

"Call them tomorrow."

July nodded. "Okay."

Paul smiled. "Well. That's good to see. You two do my heart proud. And...since you've both been doing your homework and seem to be really working on mending things with one another, I think we could move to twice a month for a little bit, then gradually ease to an as-needed basis."

"I KIND OF EXPECTED THEM TO want us to keep going longer." July kicked off her shoes and wiggled her toes. Why couldn't she go barefoot all the time?

Gareth stretched out on the bed, crossing his arms behind his head. "Me too...though I suspect they'll keep tabs on us even if we're not meeting."

July crawled onto the bed, flipping the quilt over her. Ah... bed. There was nothing like climbing into bed on a Sunday afternoon. "Probably."

"You napping?"

She rolled to her side. "I was thinking about it. That okay?"

"Can we talk about the specialist first?"

"Sure."

Gareth rolled to face her. "We *are* just getting answers right? Or are we already committed to doing whatever it takes to have a baby?"

July bristled. What kind of question was that? She opened her mouth and stopped, taking a deep breath instead of speaking. If they were working on their communication, she needed to take his questions seriously, not just react. Maybe it was a fair question. What *was* she hoping for? "Both, I guess. Though I don't really love the way you phrased the last part of the question. I don't think we'll ever be in a position to 'do whatever it takes' to have a baby. There are limits to what I'm willing to do."

"And that's why I asked. I didn't know that."

"How could you not know that? I'm not going to create tens of embryos and freeze them in the hopes of having a child. I'm not even sure I completely agree with IVF in general. I need to do more research and pray about it." She sighed. What had she done to make him lose sight of her so completely? "I'm still the same woman you married...I just want us to have a baby. That's the only thing that's changed."

Gareth was quiet for several heartbeats, his eyes fixed on hers. He nodded slowly. "Okay. So answers first? Then we'll regroup and reevaluate?"

That sounded like there was going to be a lot of time in between steps, and it left room for deciding not to have kids at all, didn't it? That wasn't an option she was willing to consider. God was going to give them children. He had to. What purpose did she have in life if she wasn't a mother? What was the point of being married without kids? Blood pounded in her ears, her chest tightening. July took a breath, willing her heart to slow. Maybe that was a discussion for another day...when it wouldn't devolve into a huge argument. "Answers first. Then...we'll see."

He pursed his lips. "Fair enough."

JULY TUGGED her sweater closed and crossed her arms. Mid-October didn't usually have this much bite in the air. Though it was just as likely to snow tomorrow as turn into Indian Summer. That was the joy of the DC area, you really never knew what you were going to get. Today, the chill suited her. If only she could've called in sick and spent the time on the porch, snuggled under a blanket with a book.

June dashed across the courtyard, tripping on an uneven brick. She narrowly avoided crashing into an older man dressed in a suit, weighed down with briefcases in each hand. "I'm late. Sorry."

July hunched further into her sweater. "Not a problem. Monday isn't our usual day."

"Everything all right?" June sat, extracting a protein bar from her coat pocket.

July shrugged. "I guess. I'm just...blue. Thought seeing you might help."

"What's up?"

"I had a weird conversation with Gareth yesterday afternoon. I'm still trying to figure out what it means." July related their discussion. "I mean, I want children...but I'm not obsessed, am I?"

"Okay, keep in mind you're talking to someone who is so hopped up on hormones right now she can barely think. And the fact that, despite said hormones, there doesn't appear to be any change whatsoever in my ovaries."

"Noted." July lifted a brow. What did that have to do with anything?

"Yes. You're obsessed. And have been for almost a year now. The first miscarriage last year shifted things. It was noticeable, at least to me. Probably also to Gareth. It's like..." June paused and stared into the sky for a moment. "Like having a child was somehow going to prove your worth and give you a purpose."

July's jaw dropped. Was it that obvious? The dark hole she'd fallen into after the first miscarriage still haunted her dreams. At least it had stopped bothering her during the day. A baby, one she could hold in her arms, would chase away the last vestiges of loss. Wouldn't it? The thought was her life raft, the only thing that kept her going some days. Tears pricked her eyes.

June's expression softened and she reached out to rub July's leg. "It's not necessarily bad...though maybe it's gone too far if it's causing problems between you and Gareth. But I understand the feeling. I've been there—still am for the most part. We're raised to believe that children are a blessing from God. The ideal Christian woman is painted as one who's at home with a brood of kids, teaching them, loving them, raising them up as the next generation. Even if she continues to work, the career woman is a mother first if she's a good Christian wife. And here we are, two women, married long enough to be established, moving up in our careers, but no kids. From the outside, it looks like our priorities are wrong and God's punishing us for it. From the inside...it's just pain."

July lowered her eyes. "I didn't think you understood."

June offered a faint smile. "In some ways I don't. I think it's harder for you because you've been pregnant and lost the baby. I imagine that feels like an additional failure."

Failure. The word made everything in July constrict. The lump in her throat made speech impossible so she nodded.

"Do you remember what you told me in the spring? That you had to choose to believe that God's plan was going to be better than yours?"

"Yeah."

"Do you still believe that?"

Did she? Her head screamed yes, but her heart...her heart just ached. "I want to."

June slid her arm around July's shoulders. "Me too."

17

June hopped onto the table and shook the thin paper sheet over her lap. At least she only had to strip from the waist down. Still, she was already completely over the frequent ultrasounds. A baby. There'd be a baby at the end of it. She squashed the tiny niggle of doubt that attempted to creep in. Positive thinking was all that kept a smile on her face these days; she'd do what she had to in order to maintain it.

A knock at the door was followed by Dr. DiCola's head peering around the edge. "All set? Great."

He scooted around the end of the table and perched on the stool in front of the ultrasound machine. As he fitted a condom full of ultrasound gel over the probe, two more men and a woman filed into the room, closing the door behind them.

June's eyes grew wide. Who were these people? Why were they in here? She tore her gaze away from the visitors and focused on the doctor. "Um. Dr. DiCola?"

"Hm? Lie back." He held up the wand and gestured for her to get into position.

She shot another glance toward the three people hanging at the end of the exam table.

Dr. DiCola frowned. "Lie back. They're just interns."

June swallowed. He was the best doctor for this. She wanted a baby. The interns were doctors too. She could do this. It couldn't—shouldn't—matter that this was now five times more people than had ever seen her naked in her adult life. She scooched down the table and turned her head away to watch the monitor.

Dr. DiCola scrunched the paper drape up, removing any semblance of modesty, and inserted the probe. Ghostly images of her ovaries and uterus appeared on the screen. A sharp pain stabbed through her abdomen as the doctor pressed the wand into her organs. The image on the screen sharpened. His lips turned down as he scrolled the mouse wheel and began to click different points on the screen. The printer on the cart began to spew grainy black and white images of her ovaries.

"You can see the classic signs of PCOS here." Dr. DiCola glanced over his shoulder and nodded to the interns. He moved the mouse along the screen, highlighting the ring of white bumps he'd shown June at her first ultrasound. They were small ovarian cysts, supposedly not harmful, though they would never form follicles. "She's done three days of follistim at 75 IUs, we upped it to 100 IUs for three days, then 150, and now we're at 250. Still no signs of follicles, though these regions look potentially promising."

The wand moved, as did the pressure in her abdomen. June winced as a stab from the other side speared through her. She took a deep breath and slowly exhaled. Why did this hurt so much? Everyone said it was supposed to be painless. The other ovary came into sharp focus on the screen and Dr. DiCola pointed out an equal lack of response. She tuned him out. He didn't seem to care that she was there anyway, and not paying attention made it easier to pretend there weren't four people she didn't know staring at her half-naked body.

Finally the probe eased out. "Go ahead and sit up. Get dressed and I'll send someone in for a blood draw."

That was it. The doctor and his crowd of interns exited the room. June smoothed the paper drape back over her lap, then leaned her elbows on her knees and buried her face in her hands. Couldn't he at least *pretend* that she was more than a random body on the table? A baby. She could put up with this for a baby.

June slid off the table and crossed the room to pull on her pants. Hopefully they'd be able to do the blood draw without digging around in her arm for a vein this time. None of the nurses she'd had so far had been any good at it. She glanced at the bruises in the crook of her right elbow. They'd probably have to try the left today. At least she'd remembered to chug two glasses of water before she came. Hopefully that would help. She grabbed her phone and climbed back on the table to wait.

"I've never felt like such a piece of meat. It was dreadful." June swallowed, blinking back tears.

Toby frowned. "That doesn't seem right. Shouldn't he have at least checked to make sure you were okay with it?"

"I would've thought so, yes." She sighed. "But what can I do?"

"At this point it's done. If it happens again, you need to say something. But for now, we need to stick out the protocol. Don't you think?"

No matter how much she wanted to run and never look back, he was right. They were in the middle of a treatment cycle, it'd be a huge waste to walk away now. "I guess. Could you come with me on Friday?"

"Let me see what time our demo starts. If I don't have to be in early, then yeah, I'll tag along. Shouldn't we be doing the procedure soon?"

June scoffed. "Sure. If my body worked like a normal person. Instead, I still have no follicles. Not even immature follicles. Nothing. No response. So I'm up to 450 IUs a day now. And he's only willing to do that dose for a max of six days."

"What does that mean?" Toby pushed his empty dinner plate away and propped his elbows on the table.

"I guess it means if we don't have any follicles next week, we scrub the cycle."

"And then?"

"I don't know. I'd imagine if he had other drugs or drug combos to try, he'd be talking about them now. If this is it and it's not working..." There had to be something, didn't there? Everyone talked about how easy it was to get pregnant with a fertility specialist because the doctors were so knowledgeable. This was supposed to be the fix. A tear leaked from the corner of her eye. Another followed. Then another. June buried her head in her hands and let the sobs engulf her, too tired to fight them back any longer.

"Hey. It's okay. We'll take it one step at a time." Toby's arms slid around her.

She turned into his shoulder and took a deep breath. His scent calmed her, slowing her tears and easing the tightness in her throat. "They're sending more medication since I'll run out tomorrow with the new, higher dose. We should check our coverage...but I think we're getting close to the limit."

He dropped his chin on the top of her head, his hands making tiny circles on her back. "Let's not worry about that right now."

"But..."

"Shh." Toby leaned back and met her gaze. "We'll think about it later. For now, let's just wait and see how things turn out. Maybe this new dosage will do the trick."

She nodded. Maybe it would. She couldn't bring herself to believe it.

18

July bounced her knee as she looked around the mostly empty waiting room. She'd been twenty minutes early in an effort to make sure she had time to get the papers completed before her appointment. And that had worked fine. But apparently, they were running late. She checked the time on her phone. Ten minutes late. Why, with a waiting room this empty, weren't they on schedule? She sighed and opened the candy swapping game everyone in the office was hooked on. She didn't consider herself addicted, but it was a fun diversion when you were stuck waiting for things.

"July?" The nurse in the doorway pronounced it like the month. Why couldn't her mother have been normal just once in her life?

July stood and gathered her things. "It's pronounced like 'Julie'."

"Oh. How original. Right this way."

July followed the nurse through a maze of hallways, finally entering a good sized room with a long, stainless steel table taking up the length of one wall. Another door opened into what looked like a bathroom. A large light hung over the table and two rolling carts with monitors and other equipment were pushed against the side of the steel table. A chair was shoved into the far corner of the room.

"Go ahead and use the restroom to completely void your bladder. Then you'll need to take off everything but your socks and put on this." The nurse offered her a pink hospital gown. "It opens in the front. You can tie the top ties if you like. Your technician will be in soon."

July waited for the click of the door before setting her purse on the chair and going into the bathroom. She locked the door and undressed. Why did she need to be completely naked? After flushing and washing her hands, she shrugged into the gown, tying the top set of ties across her chest. That wasn't too bad. At least it didn't flap open when she moved. She folded her clothes and went back into the exam room. Clutching her clothes, she perched on the edge of the chair in the corner. How long would she have to wait?

Before long, there was a knock and two nurses came in with big smiles.

The smaller nurse started speaking, her voice a chipper bubbling of sound. "Hi there. We'll be doing your HSG today. Go ahead and hop up on the table. Did they tell you what to expect?"

July shook her head.

"They never do." The nurse patted the table. The other was fiddling with the machinery on one of the carts. Clicks and chirps echoed through the room. "Basically we're going to inject dye in through your cervix. It'll go up into the fallopian tubes, then the fluoroscope here," she pointed to the machine, "will do continuous x-rays. We'll watch on the monitor and the results will be read later. We won't be able to tell you anything for sure today, but you can generally see when there's a blockage. It shouldn't hurt, though you might feel a little tingling from the dye and there could be cramps, typical of your period, afterward. Any questions?"

"No. That seems straight forward." Her mind spun. Hopefully she'd remember enough to tell Gareth about it later. But the details were already slipping away as nerves took over.

"All right, lie flat and you'll prop your heels here on the edge of the table, then slide down until your bottom is almost hanging off the table."

What was she, a contortionist? Why hadn't June mentioned this little detail? Or had she forgotten? She scooted down, her heels slipping off the edge of the table. The nurse simply smiled and repositioned her feet.

"Just a bit further."

July scooted. Pain shot through her knees and thighs. She groaned.

"I know it's not the most comfortable. But that looks good. All right, hold still. I'm going to insert the catheter with the dye. There may be a little tingle."

Fire poured through July's midsection. She bit her lip to keep from crying out. *That* was a tingle? She didn't want to know what this nurse would consider pain. The sensation turned cold. At least it didn't hurt as much. She fought the urge to squirm and turned her head to see the monitor. Blue contrast flowed through the ghostly image of her uterus and single fallopian tube. It stopped shy of her ovary.

"Hmm. Give it another little squirt." The nurse at the machine looked at the nurse with the catheter.

More fire, then cold. The image on the screen didn't change.

"All right. That's everything. Remember, you might have some cramping, and some women experience mild nausea. But otherwise, don't expect any significant side-effects. Your doctor should get the report today or tomorrow and then he'll be in touch."

With that, they shuffled out of the room.

July sat up, wrapping her arms around her waist. Hadn't they told June everything looked good? She'd have to ask what the picture had looked like. Wasn't the dye supposed to go all the way to the ovary? Her one and only tube couldn't possibly be blocked, could it? No. God wouldn't do that to her.

JULY SANK to her chin in the steaming tub. Bubbles foamed around her shoulders, teasing a tiny smile from her lips. As the heat sank into her, the muscles in her abdomen began to unclench. As the tension diminished, she opened her mouth and worked her jaw from side to side. Had she been clenching her teeth, too? Mild cramping. If that was mild, she never wanted to experience severe cramps.

"You're home early." Gareth sat on the edge of the tub and dipped a finger into the water. "Ouch. Trying to boil yourself alive?"

July chuckled. "No, just getting rid of some muscle pain that made work impossible. The water's heavenly."

"If you say so. How'd the test go?"

"I don't know. Either my nurses were tighter lipped than June's or there's something wrong. Either way, I didn't get the same 'It all looks great' speech she got. So I guess we'll wait for the doctor to call with results." She flicked some bubbles at him.

Gareth dodged, shaking his head. "You soak and simmer, I'll find something for dinner. I know it's only Thursday, but you want to put in a movie? You look like you could use it."

She had a pile of client files in her laptop bag that she'd planned to get to after dinner. But they'd keep. "You know what? That sounds perfect."

JULY THREADED her fingers through Gareth's as they checked in at the receptionist's desk. The nurse hadn't been willing to say anything other than that the doctor wanted to discuss her test results with both of them. There'd been a solid, heavy mass in July's stomach since she hung up the phone yesterday evening. Her sleep had been fitful and scarce. If the circles under Gareth's eyes were any indication, he hadn't fared much better.

He gave her hand a squeeze as they sat. Her lips curved, but weight seemed to press in on her from all sides. Why couldn't the nurse have said something useful? The door to the treatment hall creaked open, drawing July's gaze.

It was June and Toby. They looked...deflated. July drew her brows together. Shouldn't they look happy? They had to be close to their procedure...and baby. She swallowed. Was that what June had felt last year? That sinking, as if the whole world was falling out from under her? They didn't look around, just walked straight to the exit. Should she call out, say something? July eyed their slumped shoulders and hands, twined tightly together. No. There was enough time to reach out later. Maybe she'd have her own news—good or bad—to share.

"July?" Dr. DiCola gestured from the doorway. "If you'd come this way?"

They followed the doctor down the hall to his office where they'd met with him initially. He glanced at his watch as he gestured to the chairs and took his own place behind his desk.

"So we got your HSG results." Dr. DiCola flipped pages on the open folder in front of him. "You're down one tube from the ectopic in the spring, and your other tube appears to be completely blocked up near the ovary. Sometimes the HSG itself will clear out the issue, that's why they pushed some additional dye, but it didn't appear to work in this case. So IVF is your only real option. The protocol for that..."

July held up her hand. "Wait. There's nothing they can do for the tube to open it?"

Dr. DiCola's expression wasn't quite a glare. "There are surgical options, but the risks outweigh the possibility of success in my opinion. Because even if we can open the tube, the possibility of scar tissue closing it back up is high. Plus you have the recovery time from the surgery." He shook his head. "I never recommend it, especially given our success rates with in vitro."

July looked at Gareth. They hadn't really discussed IVF.

"It doesn't hurt to hear about the protocol. We don't necessarily have to do it." Gareth looked at the doctor. "Go on."

THE DIN of the restaurant made it hard for July to hear Gareth even though he was right next to her. "What?"

"I said I think I see June and Toby toward the back. Wanna see if we can join them?" He pointed across the crowded Mexican restaurant.

July followed the line of his finger and grinned. "Beats waiting over an hour. We could drive home if we wanted to wait that long before eating." She grabbed Gareth's hand and began to weave through the closely packed tables and chairs to the booth in the corner where June and Toby were poking at a basket of chips. "What are you two doing in Shirlington?"

June laughed as she looked up. "I could ask you the same thing. We actually live over here."

"Long day for me. Gareth was in meetings in Arlington today anyway, so..." July shrugged. "We haven't been here in a while and I started thinking about their tamales..."

"And that was that." Gareth shook his head. "Can we join you? They're saying it's at least an hour now, and the tamales aren't *that* good."

"Sure. Slide on in." June scooted toward the wall.

July sat next to her sister, nudging her with her shoulder. "Thanks. Did you order yet?"

"Not yet. I suspect the reason they're saying it's going to be an hour is that they only have two servers working tonight." Toby dunked a chip into salsa before turning to Gareth. "What were your meetings?"

While Gareth launched into a description of the meetings he'd been in at the National Science Foundation, July turned to June. "Saw you at the doctor this morning...you okay?"

June's shoulders sagged. "Not really. I'm just not responding to the medication. Even at the max dose for three days now I don't have any follicles forming. I'll stay at this dose through the weekend, but if there's no movement by Friday...we'll have to cancel the cycle."

July winced. After all that to have to cancel...she couldn't imagine, well, yes she could. "I'm sorry. Can I do anything?"

"Like what?" June grabbed a chip.

"I don't know. I..."

June smiled. "I appreciate the thought. What were you doing there?"

"Getting my test results." July paused when the server arrived. Everyone placed their orders and the guys continued chatting about work.

"And?" June sipped her water.

July sighed. "And my tube is completely blocked. So it's either surgery, which he doesn't recommend because of potential scarring and the recovery time, or going straight to IVF."

"What are you going to do?"

"I don't even know. We've never discussed IVF. Honestly, I'd almost rather do surgery and try naturally once the tube is clear. Though if that's what's been causing the miscarriages then, maybe not." July took a chip out of the basket and began to break it into shards. "I just don't know."

"Make sure you get him to agree to doing IVF ethically if

you decide to go that route. From what I've seen, I doubt that's his usual protocol."

July reached for another chip and began adding crumbs to the pile in front of her. "What do you mean?"

"At least when I talked to him, it sounded like he preferred to have eight or ten embryos to choose from, then he'd implant up to three with the understanding that you'd 'selectively reduce' to one if all three took."

That wasn't going to work. "I don't even like the idea of creating more than one embryo...it's still a baby."

"Yeah. I guess in some ways it's good that I don't seem to respond to the medication. It takes IVF completely out of the picture for us. I suspect I'd be tempted to do it his way, maximize the odds, even though I know better. I just want a baby so much." June leaned back as plates of steaming food were delivered to the table.

"I hear you." July used her fork to peel the cornhusk away from the luscious tamale nestled inside it and gathered a bite. "Mmm. Okay, new topic. Heard from Lydia lately?"

19

Toby ran his hand over the stubble on his chin. June was still asleep, but the way his eyes had popped open, sleep wouldn't be returning. Why couldn't his body understand the difference between weekdays and weekends? He poured coffee into his mug, shuffled to the fridge, and grabbed the half-and-half. Turning back to his coffee, his gaze landed on the bag of cupcakes they'd picked up after dinner last night. That would make a perfect breakfast.

He plopped the enormous German chocolate cupcake onto a plate and grabbed his coffee before pushing open the door to their deck. It wasn't as nice as Gareth and July's, but it was big enough for a quiet breakfast or a barbecue with a few friends. The morning chill seeped through the sleeves of his pajamas as he settled into the loveseat glider June had bought over the summer. Toby gave himself a little push to set the chair in motion before taking the first sip of liquid heaven.

He'd eavesdropped with one ear last night while June talked to July about their time at the doctor. June hadn't said much to him on their drive back to work, and even after partially focusing on her conversation with July, he couldn't figure out what she was thinking. She was upset. He could tell that much, he wasn't stupid. But that was where it ended. The doctor had mentioned using donor eggs and doing IVF. Did she want to consider that? The idea made him squirm. Didn't it, effectively, mean June would carry a child he made with another woman? Even if the process took place in a lab...he suppressed a shudder. Maybe it worked for other people, that was fine, but it wasn't something he wanted to do.

"Hey." June stepped onto the deck wrapped in a fluffy, dark green robe, a steaming mug in her hand.

"Morning." Toby moved his legs to make room on the glider. "I was just thinking about you."

"Happy thoughts, I hope?" She smiled and sat down beside him, leaning over to kiss his cheek. She wrapped both hands around the mug, pulling it closer to her face so the steam would warm it.

"Always." He took a long sip of coffee. "You ready to talk about yesterday yet?"

She sighed. "Not really. But we have to, don't we?"

"Hey." He waited until she met his gaze. "It's going to be all right. No matter what."

June leaned into him and drank from her mug. "I hope so."

"It will. Maybe we don't know what that's going to look like right now, but we'll figure it out." Toby kissed the top of her head. "Would you rather wait until we know, for sure, if we need to scrap the cycle?"

"No...we should at least figure out what our options are. Maybe...hopefully we won't have to use any of them. But...okay. So, alternative number one?" June straightened and fiddled with her mug.

Toby gave the swing another little push. "Well, the doctor mentioned donor egg IVF. That's probably what he'd consider the first, and best, alternative."

June shook her head. "I haven't researched it much yet...but

I just don't think I want that. I...can't put my finger on why. Maybe with a little more reading I'll feel differently."

"So we'll table it. For the record, I have reservations, too. I don't know what it is either, really. I don't think there's anything necessarily wrong with it, but it's just not something I think is right for us." Toby breathed a silent prayer of thanks. It was good to be, at least somewhat, on the same page. They'd spent so many months talking past and through each other when it came to their desire to have a family, this was a welcome change.

"You know, if we both have reservations, why not just rule it out? I'm comfortable saying this is God letting us know it's not right for us. My prayer since April is that we would have unity when it came to these decisions." June blew across the top of her cup before resting her head on Toby's shoulder. "In this case, we're in agreement. So, next option?"

"We can look into embryo adoption."

"Did he mention that?"

"No, but it's something I stumbled across a few weeks ago when I was looking up the various medications you're taking. Some of the medication is the same, but the focus is on getting your uterus ready to transfer an embryo rather than ovulation. Since it's just your ovaries that aren't responding, it might be an option."

June pursed her lips. "Huh. Let's put that into the category of definitely research."

Toby nodded. "I want to read more about it as well, but the little I've read sounded promising. And even if Dr. DiCola isn't willing to do it, we can probably find another specialist in the area who is. It's a growing alternative for couples who don't want to continue to store their excess embryos but who aren't willing to destroy them either."

"Cool. What's next?"

"Well." He hesitated. If only he could predict her response

before saying it. "After that, I think we're out of medical options. So it leaves us with two more choices, adoption or childlessness."

June was silent as the swing rocked gently back and forth. Toby fought the urge to fill the silence, and instead took a large gulp of coffee. She'd talk when she was ready and pushing it was never a good idea. At least he'd learned something in the years they'd been married.

"Okay." June blew out a breath. "Wow. I...wasn't ready for that. I'm not ready to give up on having a family at all yet. So, I guess if we decide embryo adoption isn't the right way to go, we look at traditional adoption. But that's not something I've considered at all...I'm not even sure where we'd start."

"Me either. But I'm glad you're not ruling it out completely." He slipped his arm around her shoulder and tugged her closer. "How about we look at embryos first, and not worry about anything else until we decide one way or another on that?"

"Sounds good." June tipped her mug and drained the last of her coffee. "I'm going to get a refill. Want one?"

"Yeah. Thanks." He handed her his mug. As the door slid shut behind her he gave the swing another little push. That had gone well. Better than most of their conversations about starting a family. It was good to have some semblance of a plan, even if it was nebulous.

20

June scrolled down the page of their fertility clinic's website. They had an embryo donation program, but the page also said the wait was over eighteen months. How current was that information? She checked the clock at the bottom of the screen; the office should still be open, even though it was Saturday. They had ultrasound appointments until noon. She grabbed the phone and dialed. After a brief conversation, June hung up and shook her head. The clinic program wasn't going to be high on her list.

Toby poked his head in the door of the office. "Were you talking to me? I was looking for something to eat and didn't hear you clearly."

"Nope. I called DiCola's office to ask about their embryo donation program. The website was pretty skimpy on details."

Toby moved from the doorway to his desk chair and leaned forward, elbows on knees. "Oh? What'd they say?"

"The wait is somewhere in the two-and-a-half year range."

Toby whistled. "That's...quite a wait."

"Yeah. It doesn't rule out embryo adoption completely, but it's not going to happen through the clinic, that's for sure."

"Want help researching?"

June shook her head. "Not yet. I know you had plans with Gareth today. Shouldn't you be upstairs getting dressed?"

"Yeah, yeah." He stopped at the doorway and cocked his head to the side. "You're sure?"

"Get out of here." She shooed at him and turned back to her computer. Since the low hanging fruit hadn't been productive, it was time to move on to a broader investigation. June wiggled her fingers over the keyboard. Where to start?

"OH THANK GOODNESS. YOU'RE HOME." Lydia glanced over her shoulder and pressed the button on her key fob. The car chirped, its lights flashing. "Please say you have time for a friend in distress."

June snickered and stepped back from the door. "Always. Though I have to ask what brings you up this way. You're a long way from home."

Lydia shrugged out of her jacket and tossed it over the stair rail before kicking off her shoes and dropping her purse on top of them. "Staci."

June's eyebrows winged up, a tiny smile tugging at her lips. "Make yourself at home. Then come on in and give me the scoop."

"Sorry." Lydia glanced at her pile of stuff in the hall. "Is there somewhere you'd rather I put them?"

"Nah. Just giving you a hard time." June headed toward the living room. "So what's Staci up to today?"

"She called my dad last week, saying *I* ditched *her*. Thankfully, she said we'd agreed to meet at a club downtown—and my dad knows that's not a place I'd go anymore—so he called her on it. Long story short, I agreed to give her one more chance for coffee this morning."

June settled on the couch. "And? She ditched you again?"

Lydia dropped into a chair. "No. She showed up. With Brad in tow."

"Yeesh. That sounds...pleasant."

"Riiiight. Pleasant is not anywhere near the word I'd use. Still, they were there so I pasted on a smile and muscled through it, even when Brad hit on me." Lydia tucked a leg under her.

"In front of his wife. Classy." June shook her head. "What did they want?"

"I still don't know. Today, at least, they're all lovey-dovey and the happiest, most wonderful couple in the world. But, here's the thing that's getting me. If Staci's in her second trimester, shouldn't she be showing at least a little by now?"

June puffed out her cheeks. Most of the women she'd seen go through pregnancy had started showing late in their first trimester, but that didn't necessarily mean it was always that way. "I'd imagine so...but I don't know for sure. I mean, you hear about those women who don't know they're pregnant and go to the ER thinking they're dying but they're really in labor."

"Yeah, all right. She's still so skinny, and they're not arguing...I didn't come out and ask, because I wasn't sure I wanted to know, but I'm kind of thinking she's not pregnant anymore."

"Ah. And I take it you're assuming that wasn't a naturally occurring circumstance?'

Lydia nodded.

June chewed on her lower lip. "I get how that would be hard for you...but I guess I'm still a little lost."

"Brad doesn't know. Or, at least, I never told him." Lydia pulled out the elastic holding her hair in a ponytail and snapped it around her wrist before running her hands through her hair.

Brad didn't know...about Lydia's abortion? Surely he'd heard about it second or third hand? Though...the gossip mill had focused much more on her car accident, drug use, and rehab stay. Had she heard about the abortion from gossip or Lydia?

"You're quiet."

June smiled. "I was thinking. I didn't think it was possible he wouldn't know but...the gossip mill at church never really focused on the abortion aspect of things. It was all about you going to rehab. And, while that's going to be a tough conversation you probably need to have with him I'm not sure how it applies right now."

Lydia seemed to shrink into herself. "Maybe it doesn't. But it makes it tough for me. I kind of feel sorry for him, and I'd gotten so used to being ambivalent about him and now..."

"Hm. Maybe before you get too worked up, you should ask Staci about it. It's entirely possible she's still pregnant and just not showing yet. Though that probably doesn't negate the fact that you're going to have to tell Brad. But...I think I'd make sure Kevin was with you. Maybe that lady at the pregnancy center too. Maureen?"

"Okay. You're right. I'm getting ahead of myself. But it brought so much rushing back and that's why I didn't want to do anything with Staci in the first place." Lydia sighed. "I'm a terrible person, aren't I?"

June scoffed. "No. You're simply a human person."

A bright smile spread across Lydia's face. "I'm so glad I bumped into you at the mall last year." She straightened in the chair and leaned forward. "What's new with you? Did you do the IUI yet? I kept thinking you'd at least text me so I could pray but...radio silence."

"No news, really." June sighed. "I'm still not responding to the drugs and I've basically got 'til Friday for that to change or we're scrapping the cycle."

"I'm sorry. Then what? You just start over?"

June shook her head. "No point. By then I'll have been at

the max dose for two weeks. If my body's not going to respond, it's not going to respond. We're starting to look at alternatives, but it's so depressing. Why does it all have to be so hard?"

"I wish I knew." Lydia rubbed her hands on her thighs. "Can I ask about the alternatives or would you rather not talk about it?"

Not talking about it wasn't really an option, was it? Wasn't that the whole point of having friends? June sighed. "We can talk about it. We've already ruled out donor egg—neither of us is really on board with it and while we can't come up with a compelling reason why that's the case...we're going with it not feeling right and stopping there."

"Makes sense."

"So right now we're focusing on donor embryos—basically people who've done IVF and end up with extra embryos donate them instead of leaving them in cold storage forever. But I spent the morning looking at it and I'm not sure it's going to be a great fit either."

Lydia furrowed her brow. "Why not? It sounds perfect? You still get to experience all of pregnancy and you, effectively, rescue a baby from being frozen indefinitely."

"That's what I thought until I started reading up on it." June rubbed the back of her neck. The statistics were terrible...and if she said them aloud it would make them real. But since she'd have to tell Toby later, maybe this could be a dress rehearsal. "It's not quite that simple. Basically, there are two ways it can work, donated embryos or embryo adoption. Donation is simpler. Far, far simpler. It's effectively a transfer of 'ownership' from one couple to another. The fertility clinic usually handles that. I called to ask about the waiting list at our clinic. It's at least two years."

"Ouch." Lydia winced.

"Yeah. So that leaves embryo adoption. And that opens up a different can of worms, cause while some people are interested in doing what they call anonymous adoption—where they give the embryos to the adoption agency to place—most people want it to work just like a traditional adoption. The biological parents of the embryo review applicants, make a choice, and have some requirements for post-birth updates and maybe even contact. And I get that, especially when you consider that the very existence of the embryos means that there are probably siblings. But...I don't know."

Lydia nodded but said nothing.

"And then you throw in the fact that you can go through all of the adoption paperwork and getting chosen—and you have to pay for all that first—then you pay for the frozen embryo transfer procedures at the fertility clinic. The first step in that process is thawing the embryo, which has an okay survival rate, but it's not guaranteed. So then, if your embryo makes it, you do the frozen embryo transfer, and then you have a thirty-five percent chance that the embryo will implant." June shook her head. "That's not particularly high."

"What happens if you don't get pregnant?"

June shrugged. "From what I can find online, it just depends. Sometimes you can adopt all of the embryos from a couple at once, sometimes it's only one. Then you have to see if there are more from that couple. If not, you start the process all over again. And it's not cheap, either."

"Huh."

"Exactly. As much as I love the idea of helping reduce the number of abandoned embryos in cold storage, that just sounds...dreadful. To go through all of that and not end up pregnant? Or what if you miscarried later on?" June swallowed, blinking back the tears that filled her eyes. "I want to be pregnant, to experience all of those things. But maybe at some point you have to decide the cost is too high?"

21

Gareth straightened and leaned on his rake, his gaze traveling to July as she mercilessly dragged at the gold and red leaves littering the yard. If they kept having so little wind in the fall, they were going to have to invest in a leaf blower. The exercise was good, and it was a nice day for it, but his back was already on fire. And there were enough trees still holding onto their leaves that they'd have to make at least one more pass at the yard later on. At least raking gave him something to focus on besides the intolerable mess of trying to have a family.

"You raking or day dreaming?" July tugged an overstuffed bag of leaves behind her toward the front of the house.

"Just waiting for you to catch up." Gareth grinned and began to scoop his leaf pile into a bag.

July shook her head. "Har-har. You're a laugh riot, Gareth."

"We all have our talents." He gathered the sides of the bag closed and gave it a twist before knotting it closed. "That should do it, don't you think?"

July stood with her hands on her hips and looked over the yard. He frowned at the calculating expression on her face.

Surely they'd done a good enough job. Okay, fine, there were still a few leaves on the ground, but really...

"Yeah, that's probably enough for now. We're going to have to do it again around Thanksgiving though, aren't we?"

Gareth nodded. That was probably about the right time-frame. He crossed the yard and reached for her rake. "Here. I'll put these away and get the last bags out to the curb for pickup if you'll make lunch."

"Seems like a fair trade. Maybe while we eat we can use the tablet to read up on IVF." July disappeared into the house before he could respond.

He hauled the bags of leaves with one hand and the rakes with the other. He should've figured out a way to make it two trips. Or three. Anything to put off more research. IVF wasn't something he wanted to do. He'd read enough research proposals that relied on, as they termed them, "excess embryos" for "test tissue"...he wasn't going to contribute to that pool. Maybe they could limit the number of eggs harvested and embryos created...even if it did dramatically lower their odds. Better to have lower odds of success than participate in something that went completely against his ethics as a Christian. Gareth sighed. It wasn't the first time his faith and his career as a scientist had been at odds. It probably wouldn't be the last. It was just the most personal the impact had ever been. He dropped the rakes in the corner of the garage and dusted his hands. Time to face the music.

He toed off his boots and left them on the steps by the kitchen door. Opening the door, grilling bread and something heavily spiced with basil filled his nose. His stomach gurgled. "That smells fantastic."

July turned from the stove and smiled. "It's just grilled cheese and tomato basil soup, but it spoke to me."

"I'll go change and wash up."

"You've got a few minutes. I just started—I wanted to run through the shower quickly, too."

Gareth took the stairs two at a time. He peeled off his clothes and dropped them in the hamper before hopping into the shower. The water was already warm thanks to July having showered. He fought the mesmerizing pounding of the hot water on his aching muscles as it tried to lull him into a relaxed stupor. With a firm mental shake, he lathered up. Done, he dried off and pulled on flannel pants and a long sleeved t-shirt. They didn't have any other plans for the day...and if July wanted to go out later, he could always change.

"So." July set a plate with a sandwich and bowl of soup down in front of him. "Initial thoughts on in-vitro?"

His stomach plummeted. *God...give me the words please.* Gareth focused on his plate, avoiding eye contact. "Why don't you go first?"

July's lips thinned. "I take it that means you're completely against it?"

"Just tell me your thoughts, okay? And we'll go from there." Gareth dunked his sandwich into the soup and took a bite.

She drummed her fingers on the table. "I want to be irritated with you...but I'm not really on board either, at least not with Dr. DiCola. Maybe another specialist would be a different story, and I guess we could explore that if you thought it would be worthwhile."

Gareth expelled the breath he was holding. It was time to tread carefully. "We can do that, if you want. I don't have anything inherently against IVF. I don't believe it's necessarily wrong, I just feel like most doctors are only worried about their statistics, not the human lives they're creating."

"Most don't think they're creating human lives. Ultimately, that's the issue, isn't it? Can you even find a fertility specialist who believes life begins at conception?" July frowned and spooned up some soup.

He pursed his lips. "That's something worth researching. There have to be some, somewhere. If nothing else, a doctor who will happily, as opposed to grudgingly, only create as many embryos as they're willing to implant."

"How many is that? Two?" July set her spoon down with a clatter. "I mean, I wouldn't really want triplets. So...two, right? Twins at the most."

Gareth nodded. Twins. Could they handle twins?

"Let me ask you this...does it really matter if he's grudging, so long as he'll do it?" July pulled a long strip of crust off her sandwich.

"Maybe not. Though I guess it boils down to how much you trust him. What's to stop him from saying he'll only make two, then creating his usual number and destroying all but the two best without telling you?"

July's eyebrows shot up. "Who would do that? That's incredibly unethical. I'd imagine he'd lose his license if he got caught."

Gareth shrugged. The 'if he got caught' was the critical part. He'd seen too many lines crossed and data fudged to maximize results at work to really trust people like Dr. DiCola. Some doctors spouted the supremacy of science above all. They were the most likely to cross lines, because they didn't have any reason not to. "Just thinking out loud. If you're not worried about it...then maybe he'd let me be in the lab and observe. I've got the qualifications."

"It can't hurt to ask. As much as I don't want to be in the 'do anything to have a baby' camp..."

Gareth studied her for several heartbeats before nodding. There it was: the baby mania. He wanted a family too, but not at the expense of his marriage or the loss of his wife. What if none of the embryos implanted? Or they did and she miscarried again anyway? When would she be satisfied and willing to concede that they needed to stop? There were other options for having a family, why couldn't they explore them? "How many?"

July frowned. "How many what?"

"How many times are we going to try IVF, assuming we can get him to agree to our terms?"

"I don't know. Do we have to decide that right now?"

"I'd like to, yes. Or at least before we get into things with the doctor. It just seems like it's a good plan to know what we're getting into before we're in it up to our necks." Gareth pushed his plate to the middle of the table.

"I guess. Let's pray about it, okay?"

He nodded. He'd pray...and do some research. Their insurance would cover the procedure, but there was an upper limit. If nothing else, that would be their cap. They absolutely would not become one of those couples in debt to their eyeballs because of their quest for a child.

22

Gareth scanned the crowd in the foyer for Toby and June. He narrowed his eyes as a familiar laugh carried across the crowded space. There they were. He wove through the clumps of people chatting in small groups or making their way to their cars.

"Hey." Gareth clapped Toby on the shoulder.

"Hey man." Toby grinned and stepped back, widening the small circle of people.

Gareth stepped into the space, nodding a greeting to Kevin and Lydia. He waited for a break in the conversation. "You busy this afternoon, Tobe?"

Toby shook his head. "We were talking about lunch, but no definite plans yet. Y'all want to come along?"

That wasn't what he had in mind, but it might work. "Maybe. I'm not sure where July wandered off to, so I'd have to check with her. Afterward...you think you'd have an hour or so? I need some computer help."

"'Course." Toby chuckled.

"Cool. I'll check with July and text you. If we can't do lunch, just let me know when you're done—or swing by."

Toby nodded and Gareth wandered back to where he'd last seen July. He found her leaning against the wall massaging her temples.

"You want to do lunch with June and Toby?"

July shook her head. "I don't think I can. My head's starting to pound. I just want to go home and lie down. Is that okay?"

"Of course, baby. Just give me a sec to let them know and we'll get you home." He tugged out his cell and tapped a quick text. Sliding the phone back in his pocket, he wrapped his arm around her waist. "Come on."

GARETH OPENED THE DOOR, but rather than motioning Toby in, he stepped out onto the porch and pulled the door shut.

"I thought you needed computer help?"

Gareth shook his head. "Nah. It was a convenient excuse to get you over here. Sorry."

"No problem. What's up?"

Gareth sat on the front step. "Pull up a seat. I need some advice."

"Okay." Toby sat.

Gareth spent a few minutes going over his conversation with July about IVF and their tentative plan. When he was done, he sighed. "I'm still not happy with it though. You know how much I want kids, and how much each loss has hit me. I'm just not sure I can take more...and the odds with IVF, especially when you do it in a way that's respectful of the lives you're creating...there are going to be more losses. But July's so set on it that I don't feel like I can say no."

Toby frowned. "That's tough. Have you talked to her about it?"

"No. I'm so tired of arguing about it...and I think it'd just devolve, rapidly, into an argument. We're doing better, but I'm having a hard time not holding my breath and waiting for the explosion."

Toby scoffed. "That's not good, man. Healthy communication isn't about not saying things that are going to upset your wife. It's about working through the problems respectfully."

"You think I don't know that?" Gareth dragged his hand through his hair. "But when you've spent the last six months getting pounded—not always unfairly, I'll concede that much—avoiding the problem looks a lot more pleasant."

One corner of Toby's mouth poked up. "Sure, it looks more pleasant, right up until it all comes spilling out, having festered for a while. Then the fight's even bigger than it would've been."

Gareth slumped. Toby was right. But what was he supposed to do about it? The entire conversation played out in his head, along with a nice little movie of July's tears, red-faced screaming, thrown objects, and slamming doors. He couldn't do it. Wouldn't. "Even knowing you're right...I just...I can't go there."

"Not sure what more I can do, man. You asked my opinion. What you do with it is up to you. But don't disregard it completely without a lot of prayer." Toby stood, tucking his hands in his pockets. "Maybe call Pastor Brown. See what he has to say about it."

Gareth lifted his hand in a casual wave as Toby drove off. He could call the pastor...but the advice would be the same. Why was it so hard to do what needed to be done?

23

"Did you get Mom's email about Thanksgiving?" June hunched into the light jacket she'd thrown on as an afterthought before heading out to lunch. She should've gone for her thicker coat. Today, at least, was definitely fall-like.

July snickered. "Yeah. Thanksgiving is what, six weeks away? And she's already trying to make plans?"

"Mmm, try four. It'll be November on Saturday."

"Four?" July furrowed her brow. "Really? Where did the fall go?"

June shook her head. "It's been a busy one, for sure. Though there's not a lot to show for it. So are you going?"

"I don't think so." July lifted her soda can to her lips and drank. "If things go right, that's when we should be finding out whether or not our in-vitro worked. I imagine we need to be at home for appointments and so forth."

"You're doing IVF? When did you decide that?"

"We talked about it this weekend. Gareth has some parameters he wants followed, but you'd said DiCola seemed grudgingly willing to change things up when you first talked to him.

So I can't see why he wouldn't do the same for us. And since it's the only real option we have for starting a family..." July shrugged.

Hadn't she said she wasn't interested in IVF at dinner on Friday? "Why the change? That's not the impression I got from you on Friday."

July huffed out a breath and crossed her arms. "Because we want to have a baby and there aren't really any other options."

"Sure there are. The same ones Toby and I are looking into. There's..."

"Just stop. I can't believe you don't understand how important this is to me. To us. Oh sure, you can throw around the idea of adopting, but have you really looked at what's involved in that? Are you really going to let someone else determine whether or not you get to have a child?" July stood and gathered her lunch. "I agree that the concerns you have about IVF are, potentially, legitimate. But that doesn't mean it's wrong, so stop being so self-righteous. You make your choice and I'll make mine."

June's mouth fell open as her sister stormed out of the courtyard. How had she been self-righteous? She'd just asked a question. And given what Toby had said when he got back Sunday afternoon, Gareth hadn't talked to July yet. Should she go after her sister? Say something? Probably not.

She bit into her apple, catching the juice with her tongue before it could dribble down her chin. She'd wanted to talk about Thanksgiving, see about inviting Mom and Dad out again this year, instead of making the trip to Chicago. If July and Gareth were going to be staying here, that made even more sense now. But last year had been so horrid...was there any reason to think it would be different? She was still fat—though at least she'd stopped gaining five pounds a month—and still had no children. Worse, she couldn't even manage to get pregnant with science helping. What would her mother say about *that*?

June sighed and tossed her apple core into the trash. She hadn't had a chance to even mention her research on embryo donation. She'd wanted to know what July thought...though if she and Gareth were going to do IVF, they were probably okay with it. As she waited for the walk light to cross Fairfax Drive, she straightened. What if...would they even consider it?

She dug her cell phone out of her pocket and punched in Toby's number as she hurried across the street.

"ARE YOU NUTS?" Toby dropped his keys on the kitchen island.

June looked up from the pot she was stirring. "Got my voicemail, I take it?"

"On the way home." He pressed his hand to her forehead. "You don't feel feverish...maybe it was a passing thing."

She smiled. Sure, the idea might be out there. But it wasn't completely crazy. "I take it that's a no, then, from you?"

He stared at her, lips parted, then shook his head. "Yes, that's a no. And honestly I'm not sure I understand how you don't realize the nightmare we'd be signing up for if we asked your sister to make extra embryos and give them to us."

"Why would it be a nightmare?" June paused her stirring. They were going to be making embryos anyway. Dr. DiCola preferred to make more than two or three. This would let him follow his preferred protocol but still keep the babies from having to be frozen or destroyed. And June and Toby's baby would be at least partially genetically related. Everybody won.

"Have you met your sister? If you carried her embryo to term, that child would never be ours. She'd second guess every single decision we made, with the reminder that, after all, we wouldn't have the baby without her." Toby paced the kitchen floor.

"Maybe. But that would be something we could discuss beforehand. Make it clear it couldn't be that way." She flipped off the stove and turned to get plates out of the cabinet.

Toby threw his arms in the air. "What if you carried to term and she miscarried? Would you give her the baby back? After all, it was hers to begin with."

"Of course not." June shot him a look. "And she'd never expect me to."

"Wouldn't she?" Toby got two glasses out of the cupboard and set them on the kitchen table.

June frowned. Did he have a point? July could be tough to deal with sometimes, but wouldn't she understand that once they'd made whatever agreement they decided on, it was irrevocable? "I don't..."

Toby cut her off. "Or what if the reverse happened? What if you miscarried? Would she blame you for the loss of her baby?"

She tried to catch her breath, but the air wouldn't fill her lungs. "You really don't like my sister, do you?"

He shook his head and got the tea pitcher out of the fridge. "I love your sister. But I don't think we want to get into a situation like that with her. The potential for insanity is simply too high."

"Insanity seems a bit harsh." June slid a plate in front of Toby and set the other at her place next to him. "I'll admit there could be some kinks, but we'd work them out ahead of time."

Toby choked on the sip of tea in his mouth. "We could try. I just don't see babies being one of the topics that stays worked out once problems arise. Best case scenario, any time you expressed even the slightest bit of frustration with our child, July'd be there reminding you that you only have him because of her and how dare you blah blah blah."

"Wow." June stabbed her fork into the chicken on her plate

and began to saw at it. Not only had he decided they were going to have a boy, though she was okay with that, he'd made her sister into a monster. "Forget I said anything."

She scooted her chair away from him, mashing her leg into the table leg. He didn't have to be so ugly about it. He could've just said no and left it at that. Well...she probably would've asked for an explanation, but it didn't have to be quite so harsh.

He sighed. "Look. I'm sorry. Maybe I'm seeing too many of the potential negatives and not enough of the positive. But since we have other alternatives...I don't see the point in opening ourselves up for that."

Other alternatives. Right. They'd have to talk about those at some point. She set her fork and knife down on her plate. Maybe now was that time, but first things first. "Since we're talking about my family and how weird they are...Mom and Dad wanted to know what we're doing for Thanksgiving."

He cleared his throat. "Um. What did you tell them?"

"I haven't said anything yet. I tried to talk to July about it, but then she got mad and stormed off. And from your response, I'm thinking I should just say we're busy."

"Did you want to go out there? I suspect my folks would love it if we did, we could see them as well."

Now wouldn't that be fun? Not that Toby's parents were bad they just...didn't like her. That was the only way to phrase it. They tolerated her because they loved Toby, but they also made it clear that she wasn't on the list of people they'd have chosen for their son. June forced a smile onto her face. "That'd be great."

Toby sighed. "They don't hate you. You know that."

"Of course I do." Hate would involve entirely too much emotion. At this point, they were resigned to her being part of the family. Which meant the barbs were somewhat more hidden in their conversations.

"Maybe we should see what my folks are up to and go from

there. It doesn't make a ton of sense, at least to me, to travel on the busiest traveling weekend of the year if we won't be able to see everyone."

"Right." June picked up her fork and pushed the food around. Hopefully his parents had already made plans. She cleared her throat. "Well, since dinner's already ruined. About those other options...I've been having second thoughts about the embryo donation adoption thing."

24

Toby looked down at his dinner and pushed the plate away. "What do you mean?"

"Donation is basically impossible unless you're willing to wait an incredibly long time. Which leaves us looking at adoption. And embryo adoption works just like infant adoption. You have to do all the same paperwork—homestudy, portfolio...and in most cases the couple who made the embryo has to actually choose you." June sighed. "And then, after all that, the probability that the baby survives the thawing process is pretty low, and the possibility that you'll have a successful implantation after that is even lower. So you go through all of that and, in most cases, you still don't end up with a baby. Not to mention the regular pregnancy risks if the embryo *does* manage to successfully implant."

He'd look up the exact numbers later, but it wasn't like the chances of conceiving naturally were all that high. Should he mention that? "Is it the odds that are bothering you, or the other stuff?"

"It's not *only* the odds. But if we're going to go through the whole process of adoption paperwork, shouldn't we be doing it for a process that's going to guarantee a baby at the end of it? I mean, we might end up waiting a while, but one way or another, if you sign up with an adoption agency you take home a child. If we sign on for embryo adoption, we take home embryos, sure...but there's still no guarantee that we end up with a baby."

"Okay. That makes sense. Are you ready to miss out on the whole pregnancy experience? I thought that was one of the primary reasons we were trying IUI to start with." Toby watched as her eyes filled with water and she turned her face away from him. He laid his hand on hers. "Hey. Talk to me."

She blinked rapidly and swallowed. "I don't know. Will I always feel like I missed out on something if I don't give birth? Maybe. Thinking seriously about closing that door is one of the hardest things I've done. But I can't get past the expense and risks with such a high potential for ending up with nothing. That just doesn't work for me."

"We don't have to decide today. You've got another ultrasound tomorrow and Friday, right?"

June nodded.

"So maybe there'll be some follicles and all this will have been for nothing." Toby leaned over and kissed her cheek. If they were going to focus on probabilities, the likelihood of finding follicles tomorrow after having no movement for so many days was tiny. But he wasn't going to remind her of that right now. She needed hope. Even if it was slim.

TOBY RIPPED OPEN the bag of candy and poured it into a large bowl. The minion hordes would be descending soon—it was almost dusk. Since June wasn't home yet, he'd get things ready, and maybe hide a few of the Snickers for himself. It had taken some convincing, but she'd finally started buying the good candy for Halloween, which made getting rid of the leftovers a lot more enjoyable. He tore open another bag and dumped it. That was good enough for a start. He gave the bowl a few shakes to mix the different varieties together and set it by the front door. The porch light was on. They were set.

Where was June? She was usually home by now, even with Friday traffic. He checked his phone. He hadn't missed any texts or calls. He frowned. He'd give her another half hour, then call. Maybe she was stopping to pick something up for dinner on the way home.

The doorbell rang. Grinning, he grabbed the candy bowl and opened the door to a chorus of "Trick or Treat!" He dropped a handful of candy into each kid's sack and waved as they thanked him and moved to the next house. He couldn't wait to take their child out. It was such a fun night. Sure, there were people who got all up in arms about it, but Toby didn't get it. It was the one day a year when it was okay to ask random people for candy. That's all his parents had ever considered it. And they could celebrate Reformation Day the morning after. He closed the door and turned.

"Boo."

He jumped, spilling a few candy bars from the bowl. Laughing, he stooped to scoop them back in. "There you are. I was just starting to wonder if I should think about worrying."

June wrapped her arms around his waist and snuggled into his shoulder. He set down the candy bowl and curled his arms around her.

"You okay?"

"Just a long day." She tilted her head up to meet his gaze. "Have you had a lot of kids already?"

Toby shook his head. "Nope. That was my second batch. Though if I had to predict right now, I'd say it's going to be a low turnout year. Not sure why, the weather's nice, but the groups are smaller."

June laughed. "I guess we'll see how accurate your prediction is. Last year you were way off base. You remember that, right?"

"Can't win 'em all." He winked. "Why was your day long? Work?"

June sighed. "Not really. I got a call from Dr. DiCola. We're done. And he even specifically said he didn't recommend trying embryo adoption. Apparently my uterus isn't responding to the medication particularly well either, so it's unlikely that we'd have a successful transfer."

Toby's heart sank. He lowered his forehead to hers. "I'm sorry."

She shrugged and blinked back tears. "You're not the one who's a failure."

"You're not a failure." He frowned, holding her gaze and willing her to absorb the full weight of his words. "I wouldn't trade you for a hundred women who could pop babies out like rabbits. So what if we can't have kids the biological way. We'll adopt."

"You aren't mad?" A tear slipped from the corner of her eye and trickled down her cheek.

"Why would I be mad? Am I disappointed? Sure. But with the drugs, not with you."

"Even though it's my fault they didn't work?" Another tear worked its way down her face.

"It isn't your fault. It's no one's fault. If I didn't produce sperm would you be mad at me? Would it be my fault that we couldn't have kids?"

She shook her head.

"Exactly." The doorbell rang. He gave her a tight squeeze. "Hold that thought while I feed some monsters."

June offered a weak smile and wandered down the hall when he released her. He turned to the door, forcing a smile for the crowd of kids thrusting out their pillowcases as they chanted "Trick or treat!"

He was halfway to the kitchen when the doorbell rang again. With a sigh he grabbed the candy bowl and answered. After he filled the bags, he waited in the doorway since another group was making its way down the sidewalk. When they got there, he filled their bags and scanned the street. The clumps of kids were all far enough away that he had a little time. He shut the door and hustled to the kitchen.

June leaned against the pantry door, staring at the contents.

"Anything worth fixing in there? I could order pizza. Or Chinese?" Toby squeezed her shoulders and began rubbing her neck.

She sighed and leaned back. "You wouldn't mind? I haven't been cooking much lately. I feel bad."

"Don't mind at all. Have a preference?"

"Dealer's choice." June shut the pantry door and glanced over her shoulder with a faint smile. "Can I put on something mindless?"

"Absolutely. Wanna see what's on the DVR or throw in a DVD?"

She gave a light shrug. "I'll see what we've recorded first."

Toby detoured to the front door to distribute more candy before calling and ordering the food. He migrated between the living room, where June was fast forwarding through some home improvement shows she'd recorded, and passing out candy to trick or treaters. By the time the food arrived, the street was practically empty of kids. He dumped a fresh bag of candy into the bowl and set it on the front step. They might just take one. Or some teenager would take it all and everyone else would be out of luck. Either way was fine with him.

He took the food to the kitchen and got out plates, splitting the pork fried rice and double cooked pork evenly between them. He dropped an egg roll on June's plate, grabbed forks and a handful of soy sauce packets, and made his way to the living room. He handed June her plate and sat, stretching his legs out in front of him.

"This okay? It's almost over." June nodded to the house hunting show she was watching.

"'Course. Did I miss the recap? I like to try and guess which one they're going to choose." He scooped a bite of rice.

"Huh-uh. Should be coming up soon though." She hit the skip button to move forward thirty seconds.

The recap of the three homes came on. Toby paused, a forkful of pork half-way to his mouth. The first was absolutely not the right one. It was too small and on a noisy street. Their facial expressions made it clear that wasn't going to be their choice. House two was nice, maybe a little on the outdated side, but it looked like easy, cosmetic fixes to him. House three was move-in ready.

"Hmm. Tough choice between two and three. What do you think they'll do?"

June shook her head. "Two. Three's too far outside their budget. She'd go for it, but he's really cost conscious."

"All right. Two it is." He grinned at her and scraped up another bite.

The couple bickered for a few minutes about the budget, but ultimately June was right and they settled on house number two. The show fast-forwarded to six months later and showcased the updates they'd made to the kitchen and master bath. Some of the changes looked easy. Maybe he should suggest a few tweaks around here. He glanced over at June.

"Good call on house two."

"It was the only real choice." She smiled and reached for his empty plate. "Here, let me take that to the kitchen. Want to throw in a movie?"

"Maybe in a minute. First...are you sure you're all right?"

She lifted a shoulder. "No. Not really. You?"

His chuckle held no humor. At least she was honest. "Maybe a little better than you, but I am disappointed. And even after our discussion on Tuesday, I wasn't prepared to lose embryo adoption as a next step. Did he explain how you weren't responding?"

"Probably, but I zoned out a little when he started yammering. You know that superior tone he gets? It drives me up a wall. And since he'd just squashed my hopes completely, I didn't feel like listening to him detail my shortcomings."

Toby rubbed a hand on her leg. "They're not shortcomings. This just isn't the way God planned for us to have a family. So we'll figure out what's next and pray about what it is we're supposed to be doing."

"Like we haven't been doing that already?" June glared. "I really thought this was what we were supposed to do. That God was going to bless it. We stepped out in faith and, wham!" She brought her hand down on her leg with a smack. "Flattened."

"I know it feels like that, but…"

"Not tonight, okay? I know you mean well. And you're right. I get that here." June touched her forehead, then her heart. "But not here."

He nodded and slid an arm around her shoulder. "Okay. Two things and I'll stop. First, I love you, no matter what. And second, we're going to figure this out."

"Thanks." June snuggled into his side.

TOBY SLID his arm under June's legs and snuggled her to his chest. She barely moved as he lifted her. She'd fallen asleep half-way through the movie they'd put in. It wasn't one he usually enjoyed, but he'd left it playing in case she awoke and wanted to see the end. She hadn't. He carried her upstairs to their room and tucked her in bed. Hopefully a good night's rest would help her gain a little perspective. Not that she should just get over it. It would take both of them some time most likely. But it was no one's fault...and it hurt that she blamed herself. He kissed her forehead and tiptoed back downstairs.

What could he do to help? The next obvious step was to research adoption. He wasn't willing to give up completely. She probably wasn't either. So if biological means of reproduction were an officially closed door...adoption it was. He wiggled his mouse to wake his computer and opened a browser. Where did you start? Typing 'adoption' into Google brought up pages and pages of results. He ignored the paid ads at the top of the screen. They might have useful information, but something less biased would be a better place to start. He clicked a promising-sounding link and began to read. After a moment, he opened a desk drawer, grabbed a notepad, and began taking notes.

Who knew there were so many options?

25

July paced in the courtyard. Would June come? They hadn't spoken since last week. Heat burned her cheeks and a leaden weight settled in the pit of her stomach. She owed her sister an apology.

It was a deceptively sunny day. The cold air wormed its way through her jacket when she stood still. The benches were filling with people looking to seize one of the final days of nice weather before the winter cold took a firm hold on the region. Stuffing her hands in her pockets, July perched on the edge of a bench to stake her claim.

June stopped at the edge of the courtyard. July lifted a hand.

"You'd never know it was this cold from looking out the window." June shivered as she sat. "We're going to have to decide on our restaurant of choice before too long."

"That's a plan. I, uh, wanted to apologize. For Tuesday." July rubbed her arms.

"Don't worry about it."

July pressed her lips together. Was her sister just humoring her? "I shouldn't have said you were being self-righteous. You were just asking a question. A fair one, at that."

"Thanks. But you were right, to some degree. It's not my business. If you and Gareth are comfortable, then it's what you should do. Especially if you can get Dr. DiCola to work within your limitations. I just hope it works for you."

"What about you? Aren't you doing your procedure soon?"

June shook her head. "Scrubbed the cycle on Friday. And basically got the thank you for playing speech from the doctor. He didn't even recommend trying embryo adoption, which was going to be our next step. So...now we're starting to look into adoption."

Adoption? July cleared her throat. "I owe you another apology for that, as well. You know I'm pro-adoption. Right?"

June waved away July's words. "You were upset. I was upset. It's okay. I...at this point I'm starting to accept that Toby and I aren't going to be the only people involved in us having a family. That was true even when we were hoping to conceive with IUI. But now? We're just praying and trusting that God will bring the right baby to us."

Just like that? Just step back and trust that God was going to do it? It was a great thought, but how did you get to the point that it was something you could actually *do*? "You make it sound easy."

"Ha. No, it's not easy. I wouldn't even say we're doing particularly well with it. Well, I'm not. Toby's much better at it than I am."

"He's always been more laid back than you." July grinned.

"Too true. So, he's trusting and hanging back. I'm researching. Though I did notice he'd been jotting down adoption information—so he's been doing some research too. It helps, sort of, to have a new focus. Eases the sting of the failed cycle a little. What about you? When will you start your IVF cycle?"

July frowned. "This week. I go in tomorrow to get all the protocol details. Gareth wants a clear promise on how many times we're going to try before we give up, but...I don't know how to decide that."

"What's your gut say? Any instinct?"

"Not really." July shook her head. "I get the feeling that Gareth wants me to say we'll only try once. But...then what? I think it's great that you and Toby are in agreement about adoption, but I don't see that happening for us. So where does that leave us if this doesn't work?"

June furrowed her brow. "You really don't think Gareth would adopt? I've always felt he'd be on board with that if it's what you wanted."

And that was the crux of the matter right there. As much as she wanted a family, adoption was never something she'd felt called to. She couldn't put her finger on it, but the idea of her children not being biologically hers just wasn't something she could handle.

"Oh." June looked down at her hands. "It's not Gareth who's the problem. Does he know?"

July shook her head. "We've never really talked about it. He mentioned it a few times after the miscarriage last fall. Then again after I lost my tube. I keep waiting for him to bring it up again...but so far he hasn't. And I don't want him to. I can't explain my problem—difficulty, it's not really a problem. I don't even know how to try."

"Well...hopefully you won't have to." June offered a tight smile as she stood. "I need to get back. We've got a deliverable this week and, as usual, we're behind. Plus, Lydia texted this morning and is hoping I can meet her for dinner tonight. I told her I'd try. But we'll have to see how things go getting this code up and running."

"Okay. Thanks for coming out. I love you. You know that, right?" July tucked her hands in her pockets.

"Yeah. Back atcha." June winked.

July watched her hurry across the courtyard and disappear

behind the office building. That could've gone better. Though at least June had accepted her apology. That was something. Of course, the adoption conversation had driven another wedge into their relationship. Why couldn't anything ever be easy?

"CAN I ASK YOU SOMETHING?" July hit pause on the remote, freezing the screen with a modern-day Sherlock Holmes in mid-word. How did she always manage to catch people with their mouths open?

"Sure." Gareth shifted on the couch to face her. "What's up?"

"So I was talking to June today and the way she said something...I'm probably reading into it...but it keeps popping into my head, so I'm just going to ask."

"Okay?"

July exhaled loudly. Why was this so difficult? "You're on board—really, truly, one-hundred-percent on board—with the decision to try IVF. Right?"

Gareth pursed his lips. "I'm on board. Yes. One-hundred-percent? I don't know. I have reservations. I'm trying to get past them because you've got your heart set on this. And I understand wanting to explore every possible medical option before we move to adoption. But if you look at the odds, I can't help thinking we'd be better off in terms of time and money if we just moved on."

July licked her lips as her stomach plummeted. How had she misinterpreted his feelings so drastically? "You don't have any expectation that it'll work? People do get pregnant from IVF, you know that, right?"

"Of course I do. You don't have to get defensive. I told you I was on board—but I'm not going to lie and say I'm excited about it. We'll try it and see how it goes. If it works, awesome.

But if it doesn't, are you going to be willing to look at other options?"

She swallowed. Adoption. She shrunk into herself. He was going to hate her. But it was better to get it out in the open, wasn't it? "Um. I...no. I'm sorry. But I..."

"What?" Gareth exploded off the couch, hands flying into the air. "We talked about this before we got married. You know I've always loved the idea of adoption—especially if we can adopt an orphan from another country. Someone who needs us, who we can not only love, but give a better life. You said you understood that."

"I do understand it. I just don't necessarily agree with it."

"So, what...you lied to me because you realized it was important to me? That it could well end up being a deal breaker for our relationship?" He shook his head, a mixture of disbelief and disgust evident on his features.

"I didn't lie. If we had our own children, I'd be on board with adding to our family through adoption. But I want at least one of our kids to be wholly ours, not some kind of long-term mission project."

His mouth fell open. "How...what..." He shook his head and stalked into the kitchen. "I'm going out for a bit. Don't wait up."

The door slammed. July jumped. That hadn't gone well. She stared at the ceiling. The problem, well one of the problems, was that she saw where he was coming from. Sort of. He was trying to get over his reservations about IVF for her...why couldn't she do the same about adoption for him? Maybe she could. If she had to. And if he'd give her the chance.

She reached for the phone and punched in the Brown's number. Clearly she and Gareth needed to spend more time with them.

26

Gareth pulled to the curb in front of the pastor's house. He hadn't realized where he was driving until he turned onto their street. Now...he might as well see if they were busy. He checked the clock on his dashboard. It was just after seven-thirty. Not too late. He got out of the car, tucked his hands in his pockets, and headed up the walk.

What was he hoping to accomplish?

He sighed and poked the doorbell. If nothing else, maybe they'd pray with him.

Mary beamed and opened the door wide. "Gareth. How lovely to see you. Come on in."

"I'm sorry for interrupting your evening." He hesitated on the threshold. "I should just go."

"Nonsense. We were actually hoping you'd find your way here." She offered a sympathetic smile. "July called."

Of course she did. He sighed and stepped through the door. "Then I guess you know everything."

"Not really. She just mentioned that you'd had an argument and you had left to clear your head. She wasn't sure if you'd end up here, but she was hopeful that you would. She also asked if

I'd tell you that she was going to work on getting past her objections. And I'm hoping you won't mind filling us in." Mary had led the way to the family room as she spoke and gestured to the sofa. "Have a seat. Can I get you something to drink?"

"I'm fine. Thanks." Gareth sat, nodding hello to Paul.

Paul slipped a bookmark between the pages of a thick tome and set it aside before lowering the footrest of his recliner. A slight smile tugged at his lips. "Eventful evening, I gather."

Gareth pinched the bridge of his nose. "That's one way to look at it."

"Could you fill us in? July said she was fine with that, if you were concerned." Mary settled into an arm chair and crossed her ankles.

Why not? Wasn't that why he was here in the first place? Sub-consciously, at least, he must have wanted to talk to them. He sat back, the whole story pouring out of him. Finished, he scrubbed a hand over his face. "I just don't understand how she didn't think it was important to explain that she wasn't on board with the idea of adopting regardless of our biological child status."

Paul was silent for the space of several heartbeats. "First, I just want to say I'm impressed that you talked about adopting at all prior to getting married. Most couples only talk about kids in the generic 'do you want them' terms. Honestly, my premarital counseling has primarily focused on that as well. I'm beginning to see that facing the idea of infertility head-on, from the beginning, might not be a bad thing."

Gareth frowned. What was he getting at? Did he mean that July wasn't wrong to have kept that little tidbit to herself? That somehow he should've known to clarify that he wanted to adopt regardless of whether or not they had biological kids? Though, in the end...wasn't he saying July should have known she needed to clarify her position? He sighed.

"That said." Paul cleared his throat. "I have a hard time

faulting July for not fully explaining her thoughts when you talked about it. I don't think any young person seriously considers that they might not be able to conceive when they want to. If they did, I suspect more couples would be starting their families early in their marriages instead of waiting until age has diminished their fertility."

"Yeah...I came to the conclusion about July while you were talking. It's just so hard, because I have serious qualms about doing IVF, but I'm pushing them aside, or trying to, since her heart is set on it and she seems to think it's what God's leading us to do. But...it just doesn't seem like she's willing to do the same for me."

"I believe she is." Mary leaned forward. "I definitely got that impression, at least, from her phone call."

Gareth nodded. Maybe.

"I think, at this point, you should go forward with your current plan, since those wheels are in motion. And that will give both of you time to keep praying about adoption and where it fits in God's plan for your family." Paul pursed his lips. "And try to be gentle with one another in the meantime. This treatment is going to be rough, emotionally. If only because of the hormones July will be on. Our eldest daughter and her husband went through a similar treatment for their first child. It was rough. Try to remember why you're together in the first place—don't lose sight of who you are as a couple in your quest to define who you are as a family."

"All right." Gareth clasped his hands in his lap. When had they lost sight of who they were as a couple? Last year, after the first miscarriage? That's certainly when things started to shift—when having a baby took control of their lives. They needed to reclaim some of their joy in coupledom. But how? "Any suggestions on how to do that?"

"Can you get away for a weekend? Or even just a nice date? Think about what you used to do, when you were courting or newly married." Mary smiled. "It doesn't have to be extravagant. It just needs to be the two of you."

"HEY." Gareth sat on the bed next to July and caressed her hair. "Thanks for calling the Browns. How'd you know I'd end up there?"

She set her e-reader down. "I didn't. But I hoped you would." She cleared her throat. "I'm sorry."

"No. I'm sorry. I made assumptions and got upset when they were proved wrong. But that's not your fault. You didn't lie. And as long as you're willing to pray about it with me...we'll figure it out."

She nodded. "We will. I'm sure of it."

He kissed her head. "I'm going to play a game on the computer for a bit, if that's okay?"

"Sure. I'll probably turn out the light in a chapter or two."

"Okay. Night. I love you."

"Love you, too." She smiled and picked up her e-reader.

Gareth made his way downstairs and booted up his machine. He did plan to play, but first he was going to look into a weekend away. Maybe a trip up to Lancaster? They'd done that once, when they were first married. It had been a fun weekend of shopping, good food, and sightseeing. The best part was it was just a couple of hours drive. With Veteran's Day approaching, they could take a three-day weekend relatively easily. If he could still get reservations somewhere.

He scanned the first page of bed and breakfast search results, opening a few of the options in new tabs for more in-depth consideration. Should he check with July first? Make sure she was up for it? She didn't always love surprises...but she did okay with them. Nah. He'd take the chance.

27

"Thanks for coming. I know you don't usually come to church on Wednesday night, but it was the only time I could figure out that would work for everyone." Lydia gave June a fast hug.

"It's not a problem. Toby was happy to hang with Kevin for a bit." She looked around. "Where'd the boys go?"

"Probably getting Brad. This thing with Staci has turned into a huge mess and I'm not sure what else to do. So, I asked Maureen to come and she and my dad are going to talk to Brad and Staci together, see if they can't get it sorted once and for all."

"Okay...why do I need to be here? Or you, for that matter?" June kneaded the back of her neck.

Lydia cleared her throat. "We're sort of moral support."

"For who?"

"Staci."

June's eyebrows shot up. "Really? How'd that happen?"

Lydia shook her head. "All I know for sure is Brad convinced her to abort the baby if she wanted to stay married. He denied it was his—still does, honestly. Saying he's not able to have kids. But since I know better, first hand, and he knows that I wasn't sleeping around when we were together..."

"And Toby and me? Why are we here?"

"For afterward...when I'm pretty sure Kevin and I are going to need a friend. I'm hoping between after-abortion counseling and marriage counseling, Maureen and Dad can get them headed on the right path. But...part of me wants to see them implode. And I knew you and Toby wouldn't think worse of me because of that."

June shook her head. "Of course not...honestly I'm not sure I want to see them stay together either. Why are the people who need us to show them the love of Christ so often the ones who are impossible to love?"

Lydia offered a sardonic smile. "That's the question, isn't it?" She checked her phone. "That's my dad's signal. Pray for us, would you? I'll find you when we're done."

At least she didn't have to sit in the meeting with them. June made her way to the small chapel off the side of the main sanctuary and took a seat in a pew. She lowered her head to her clasped hands and searched for the words to pray. Why did God allow people to have children and throw them away? It wasn't fair. But fair wasn't something they were promised. Still...on the other hand, could she do a better job than God? She scoffed. She didn't even want to try.

Toby slid into the pew next to her. "Did Lydia fill you in?"

June nodded.

"It's hard to accept people who have just thrown away a baby. Even though they're not friends I just don't understand it. And then to know that not only will God forgive them, if they ask, but that we need to...well, I'm struggling."

She dropped her head on his shoulder. "I'm glad I'm not the only one. That's what I was just thinking about...trying to pray about, though I couldn't find the words."

He smiled and kissed the top of her head.

They sat like that for a while until Kevin came and tapped June on the shoulder.

"Could you go check on Lyd for me? She's in the ladies room in the hall. The meeting's over. It...didn't go well. Brad and Staci are headed for divorce, Brad's under church discipline, and Staci...I'm concerned about her but not sure what more we can do. I think Maureen's going to try to keep an eye on her."

June's eyes grew wide and she slipped from the pew out into the hall. That hadn't been an outcome she'd even considered. Why hadn't God fixed things? Drawn them to Him? Saved their marriage? He was capable...but He didn't force His will on people. Still, how stubborn did you have to be to resist it when so many people tried to help?

She knocked on the door to the far stall. "Lydia? You all right?"

"No." She sniffled. "I'd forgotten how hateful Brad could be when he got mad."

The stall door creaked open. Lydia came out, tears streaming down her face. She went to the sinks and splashed water on her face.

June rubbed Lydia's shoulder. "Sorry. What can I do?"

"Nothing." Lydia swiped her hands over her face. "There's nothing anyone can do but pray. I shouldn't have asked you to come. I...I thought it was going to be bad, but not that bad. I hoped we could go with you and Toby to get some dessert afterward. Now...I just want to go home."

"Okay. Call me if you think of a way for me to help."

"How did you do it?"

June looked at her sister over the top of her soda bottle. "Do what?"

"Give yourself shots every day? I'm only three days in and I'm already dreading each dose. It doesn't hurt, exactly, but..."

June chuckled. "I hear ya'. You get used to it. It helped me to remember why I was doing it. Have you had an ultrasound yet?"

"This morning." July began unloading the contents of her lunch sack.

"And?" Given that her sister wasn't saying anything, she probably had follicles coming out the wazoo.

July shrugged. "Things seem to be developing like they should. Dr. DiCola was pleased. He thinks we should be able to do a retrieval on the fourteenth."

"That's great." June forced her mouth into a smile. It *was* good. If it had to work for someone, at least it was her sister. Maybe a niece or nephew would ease the pain of the choices people like Brad and Staci made.

"I shouldn't tell you about it. I'm sorry." July sighed. "This is going to be awkward, like last year, isn't it?"

June shook her head and rested her hand on her sister's knee. "No. It's fine. I really am happy for you. Does it hurt a little that it's working for you so quickly? Yeah. But that doesn't mean I don't want to hear about it. I'm happy for you. Even when I'm upset for myself."

"You're sure?"

"I'm sure." June screwed the lid back on her soda. "Hey. Toby and I are going to an adoption information session on Monday. Wanna come along? I know it's not your plan right now, but I thought..."

"Maybe. Lemme talk to Gareth and see what he has planned. You know how he gets on those home improvement kicks when three-day weekends roll around." Half of her mouth quirked into a smile.

"True. Ah the joys of home ownership." June focused on the fact that her sister hadn't dismissed it completely out of hand.

That was a positive step. She hadn't even confirmed with Toby that they were going, so it bought her time to do that as well. Who knew what projects he might have already lined up for the weekend? He got the same bug Gareth did most of the time.

"Where were you last night? Mom called my house looking for you. She said you still haven't said one way or the other about Thanksgiving. Are you going?"

Ugh. Thanksgiving. Her insides twisted. "Toby said if we go we could see his folks too. I got considerably less excited about the trip when he mentioned that. So we'll see. I guess I need to push him to make a decision though. As for last night..."

June filled her sister in on the excursion to church and the results.

July wrinkled her nose. "Yuck. That sounds...uncomfortable. For everyone."

June nodded. "I'm a little worried about Lydia. Can you get PTSD from something like that? Maybe that's too severe, but she was really torn up."

"I don't know. Should we see if she wants to hang out on Friday? Maybe that'd cheer her up?"

"Hm. That's not a bad idea. Let me run it by her and I'll text you tonight." June glanced at the time on her phone. "I should run. Seems like Bob is scheduling meetings closer and closer to lunchtime. I don't want to be late."

28

"Do we have plans this weekend?" July dropped onto the sofa next to Gareth and glanced at the television. The TV host, Mike Holmes, was busily tearing out a leaking sink. The sound was muted, but she suspected he was in the process of lambasting the contractor who'd done a poor job of installing it in the first place.

"Um...why?" Gareth looked away from the screen, his gaze meeting hers.

July sighed. "Couple of things. June was thinking maybe we ought to see if Lydia wanted to hang out tomorrow night. She's had a rough week."

"That might work."

"And...June invited us to an adoption seminar on Monday."

Gareth's eyebrows lifted. "You didn't laugh her out of the courtyard?"

Her lips thinned. "I said I'd try to get over my objections. I thought you'd be thrilled that I was asking you about it. I'll just tell her no."

He laid a hand on her leg. "Wait. I'm sorry. You're right. I'm just surprised. And now I have to decide what to do."

"What do you mean?"

"I was going to surprise you...Paul and Mary suggested that we make sure that we weren't losing sight of ourselves as a couple. That this quest for us to have a child hasn't become our sole reason for being married." He met and held her gaze. "It isn't. Even if we end up childless, I'll always want to be married to you. I can see how you might question that based on how things have gone lately...and I don't want you to think that way."

Childless. A shiver wriggled down her spine. Could they really end up childless? Would they survive it if they did? Could they? She swallowed. The specter of having no children lingered in her mind but she forced brightness into her tone. "What does that have to do with a surprise?"

He drummed his fingers on his knee. "I guess I might as well tell you. Then you can decide what we do. I made reservations in Lancaster at a B&B. I thought we'd spend the weekend roaming the farmland. Maybe get something for the garden or one of those quilts you're always admiring. Or nothing but shoo fly pie and homemade birch beer. Either way, just take a break and simply be with one another."

Her spirit lightened. "That sounds lovely. Tell you what. I'll get the details from June about the seminar—it's probably a good idea for us to go to one, no matter what happens with this cycle of IVF. But they're bound to do it more than once a year, right? So we'll plan on another time. When do we leave?"

Gareth chuckled. "I was thinking tomorrow after work, but if you want to hang with Lydia, I can see about cancelling that night of our reservation."

She shook her head. "Don't. Some us time sounds like just what the doctor ordered. And as bad as I feel about Lydia right now...I think maybe it's better, in this case, to be selfish."

"You're sure?"

"I'm sure." She glanced at the time on the DVD player

above the TV. "Let me just give the doctor's office a quick call and make sure we're good as far as ultrasounds. We should be, but..."

"It's good to double check." Gareth nodded and hit the mute button, filling the air with Mike Holmes' voice explaining the benefits of spray foam insulation.

JULY KICKED the suitcase out of the way and pulled open the freezer. She dumped ice into the tiny cooler and opened the fridge. The medication should be fine for the trip—it wasn't that far. The B&B would hopefully let her store it in their fridge. Or at least let her have some ice to keep it chilled. Maybe this trip was a bad idea. She dropped the syringes into the cooler and snapped it closed. She and Gareth needed the time together but...retrieval was likely going to be in a week. Possibly less if the follicles continued to develop like they were. Her ultrasound this morning had been very promising and Dr. DiCola had seemed reluctant to miss the ultrasound on Monday. But ultimately he'd given the okay. So it was going to be fine.

"Ready?" Gareth poked his head through the kitchen door and grabbed her suitcase.

"Yeah, that's everything. I'm going to make one more run through to be sure all the lights are off, doors locked—you know the drill. Then I'm set."

He nodded and pulled the door closed. She hefted the cooler. Medicine, check. A quick zip through the house found everything in order. July pressed a hand to her stomach to quell the grasshoppers jumping up and down in it. This was ridiculous. It was a weekend away with her husband. It wasn't as if they were newlyweds.

She tugged the kitchen door closed behind her and gave the

handle one more twist to see that it was locked. She slid into the passenger seat and tucked the cooler between her feet. "All right. Let's go."

THE DRIVE HAD BEEN as uneventful as it could be given that they still had to deal with the Beltway and it was the Friday afternoon of a three-day weekend. Still, they got to the B&B only a half-hour past the arrival time they'd given. The owner showed them to their room and confirmed breakfast for eight thirty the next morning.

July looked around. It was an adorable set-up. Their room had probably started out as the screened in porch – and maybe part of the main house as well. The front area held a queen-sized bed fitted with what could only be an Amish quilt and lots of pillows. Rough planks lined the walls, making the space cozy and rustic. A loveseat lined the wall just inside the door and a tiny television DVD player combo perched atop a mini-fridge to the door's other side. She tugged open the door of the fridge and tucked her medication on the top shelf next to some sodas.

A hall split the back wall between the couch and the bed. July followed it, trailing her fingers lightly across the rough boards. A door on the right led to a small full bathroom. The hall ended just beyond the bathroom door with an open closet. There was a suitcase stand positioned under a hanging bar and hangers. Shelves holding extra towels and toiletries were recessed into one side wall.

"This place is delightful. How'd you find it?" July leaned back so she could see down the hall where Gareth was poking around in the fridge.

He laughed. "Google and luck. They have a great website— and their pictures actually match what you get, so that's nice.

When I saw this room, kind of separate from the rest of the more typical B&B guest rooms, I knew it was where we needed to be. The little guest cabin looking thing across from the pool? You can rent it, too, if you've got four or six people. Maybe we should see if Toby and June want to come up sometime together."

"That'd be fun." She wandered back down the hall and took off her shoes, tucking them out of the main walkway then flopped backward onto the bed. "Comfy."

"Tired already? I was thinking we could find a place to have some dinner. That's the one downside of this place, we're not really within walking distance of anything. But I'm sure there's a place close enough that we wouldn't be driving for long."

"Dinner sounds good. Why don't you go to the main house and get a recommendation and I'll rest for a few minutes."

29

The quiet chirp of the car doors locking echoed through the nearly empty parking lot. The practically empty state of the lot in the deepening twilight was all that indicated the brick townhouses were businesses, not homes. Soft yellow light pooled at the bases of old-fashioned lamps, though many areas stayed shrouded in gloom.

In silence, June and Toby walked between two rows of townhomes, looking for the door they needed. What was he thinking?

Toby stopped and tugged open a green door. "Here we are."

June followed him into the small foyer and frowned. There were locked doors to either side, each with a small plaque displaying a business name. Directly in front of them were five steps leading to a wide landing, but the ceiling sloped overhead, so it was clear the stairs continued after the landing turned. On the wall of the landing was another brass plaque, this time with the adoption agency's name and an arrow pointing up.

She pointed. "Upstairs, I guess."

"Yep."

They took the stairs slowly. Her fingers tightened in Toby's. It was comforting that his squeezed back as hard as they did. Maybe he was nervous after all.

At the top of the stairs was a long hallway. Quiet chatter drifted toward them from the far end. June fought the urge to tiptoe past the dark offices on either side of the hall. Finally they reached an open area where four other couples gathered in a loose circle, chatting.

"Can I help you?" A slim woman, probably in her mid-fifties, smiled at them from behind a desk.

"We're Toby and June. We signed up for the information meeting?"

"Of course. Welcome." The woman clapped her hands for attention and ushered everyone into a room off to the side. There were couches and arm chairs in a circle, almost like a living room or den. Bookcases filled with binders, the titles prominently featuring the word "adoption", lined one wall.

June and Toby squeezed onto one half of a couch, leaving nearly a full cushion between them and the other couple who shared the space. June offered a tight smile before focusing on the woman from the agency as she settled into an arm chair, a stack of folders on her lap.

"I'm so glad you all were willing to take time out of a three-day weekend to come to our informational session. I'm Faith Michaelson, the director here in our Fairfax office. In addition to keeping things running day-to-day, I'm also one of the primary birthparent liaisons. So I have the privilege of talking with these women, and sometimes men, as they come into the agency to explore placing their child. We'll talk more about that as we go along tonight. However, our agency also has an international adoption program and I'll start with details about that program." She paused and took a sheaf of papers out of the top folder on her lap. She handed the stack to the couple sitting on her right. "Take one and pass the rest, would you please?"

June watched the papers make their way around the room. Why didn't they separate their information sessions into domestic and international? She took one of the packets and glanced down at it. The list of countries the agency worked with was long—but none of them offered infants. She might not be able to experience pregnancy and childbirth, but she still needed the infant experience. Shaking her head, she handed Toby the packet as Faith began to speak.

"As you can see, we work with a number of countries internationally. The worldwide adoption arena is one that's constantly changing. Some of our programs are currently not accepting new applications as those countries take a closer look at their adoption requirements and consider joining the Hague Convention. Other countries that used to be fairly easy to adopt from have significantly changed, and the wait times have lengthened in response. Ten years ago, international adoption was a difficult process to navigate, but the outcomes were guaranteed and timely. Today, the process is considerably easier, the outcome mostly guaranteed, but the days of making it home with a child in under a year are, for the most part, a thing of the past."

June fidgeted. This wasn't anything she cared about. She and Toby weren't going to adopt internationally...they wanted an infant. Her mind wandered as Faith continued to speak in more depth about each country, the application process, and what couples could expect from the process.

"Any questions?" Faith glanced around the room. "No? Okay. Let's take a quick break—feel free to grab some more coffee or a soda from the main room out there. Restrooms are back down the hall, near the stairs."

June glanced at her phone. Forty minutes. Even longer than she'd thought. She stood, stretching, and followed Toby out into the main area.

"You ready to go?" Toby tapped the packet of information

against his hand. "We've got enough to get started. I'm sure glad she started with international...saves us having to sit through a ton of information that doesn't apply."

"What do you mean? We're not..." June shook her head. "I thought...a baby, Toby. I want a baby. Not a two year old."

He frowned. "Really? That's one of the best things about adopting, you can skip the late night feedings, teething..."

"I don't want to skip those things. I don't really want to miss out on pregnancy and delivery, but that's been taken out of my hands. I'm not giving up anything else." How did he not understand that?

Toby rubbed the back of his neck. "Oookay. I just assumed..." He shrugged. "That's fine. We'll stay and get the rest of the information. Maybe once we've heard about both sides, we'll be able to make our decision more clearly."

June shot him a look. There wasn't anything unclear about the decision now. Except that he wasn't paying attention.

Faith called everyone back to the room.

"I'm passing around our domestic adoption packet now, please take one per couple and pass them along. While the national headquarters handles the bulk of our international adoptions, we generally handle the domestic adoptions at our local offices. So since you're all in the Northern Virginia area, we'd handle your application and placement locally. If you want to broaden your search, you can choose to have your profile shared on our national website and put in that database. It does add a few extra steps to the adoption process as you'll have to work through the Interstate Compact for the Protection of Children as part of placement. This is easy enough to do, it's just extra paperwork." Faith smiled and opened the folder on her lap. "Now, if you'll all please look in the left pocket of your folders?"

∾

JUNE CLUTCHED the folder of information and glanced over at Toby as he navigated through the parking lot back out to the main road. She cleared her throat. "What'd you think?"

He glanced over with a light shrug. "Seemed pretty straight forward—and in line with the research I've been doing. I guess we never actually talked about domestic versus international."

Hadn't they? She wracked her brain. "I guess not. I was sure we had. How set on international are you?"

"I'm not. I thought it was what you wanted." He glanced over with a grin. "I'm fine either way. I just want you to be happy. Though..."

"What?"

"I guess I was thinking international because you really do have a guarantee. I mean, sure, you wait—and those waits look like they range anywhere from eighteen months to more than four years depending on the country—but you always, always end up with a kid at the end of it. Domestic seems...capricious, I guess."

Capricious? "How so?"

Toby sighed. "I don't know. There's just no guarantee for anything. You could wait three weeks or three years or even more. You could just wait and wait and wait and never be chosen at all. You don't get any say in it once your application is in and your portfolio is put together."

She cocked her head to the side. That was true...she hadn't looked at it like that. "Okay. I guess I see that. But, for me at least, the chance to have a newborn, to take him or her home from the hospital...I'm willing to take that risk."

He pursed his lips and they drove in silence for several minutes. "You're sure?"

"Yeah." Should she mention that the cost of domestic was less than international? That wasn't the deciding factor, obviously, but it was a factor. Wasn't it?

He licked his lips. "All right. Domestic it is."

30

"How was your weekend?" June scooted her chair closer to the table in the crowded coffee shop to clear more room for people trying to get by.

July smiled and leaned back. "Really nice. The B&B Gareth chose was delightful. We had a room that was separate from the majority of the guests, so it felt more like being at home than in a hotel. The food...wow, the woman who owns the place is a fantastic cook. Our breakfasts were so filling we ended up skipping lunch most days and just having dinner a little early."

"Sounds nice. What'd you do during the day?" June had often looked at Lancaster as a place to visit, but never really figured out what there was to do.

"Wandered around the shopping areas, mostly. There are so many different craftspeople—from quilts and wooden objects to farm stands...there's a lot to see. And we were able to get tickets to the Sight and Sound Theater. That alone would make the trip worthwhile. Plus, we stumbled across a life-sized replica of the Tabernacle. That was interesting."

"The Tabernacle? As in the Israelites? That Tabernacle?"

July nodded. "Like I said, it's interesting. They have one whole wall missing so you walk down and look in at the Holy Place where you can see the showbread and the candelabras. Then the curtain that separates the Holy of Holies. But you get to look in, and see the Ark of the Covenant. I've never spent a ton of time really imagining what it looked like, so it was neat."

"Huh. Sounds like it. Maybe we'll have to take a trip that way sometime."

"If you do, let us know. The B&B has a cottage you can book. It sleeps four to six. Might be fun to make it a sibling trip."

"Speaking of sibling trips..." June took a long drink from her soda. "I guess we're going to end up in Chicago for Thanksgiving after all. Any chance you all can come?"

July pursed her lips. "IVF-wise, we probably could make it. I'll be doing the trigger shot this afternoon when I get home. So they'll do retrieval on Friday and embryo transfer sometime next week, maybe Tuesday or Wednesday, depending on how they're growing. So...we could. But I'm really not sure I want to."

June chuckled. "Gee. Why not?"

"Maybe because I haven't actually told Mom that we're doing IVF? You know how she feels about it, right?"

"Yeah. I got the whole song and dance when I said we were trying IUI." June frowned. "You really haven't told her?"

July shook her head. "I guess I should...have you told her about moving on to adoption?"

June groaned. "No. I don't want to, either. I know we're going to have to...I guess we can save that for an in-person conversation around Thanksgiving dinner. And we can also tell Toby's folks while we're visiting. Though they, at least, will probably not say anything nasty."

∾

JUNE STARED at the adoption application. Who thought up these questions? The first two pages were standard names and addresses, much like you filled out for a security clearance. In fact, she'd pulled out her clearance paperwork to double check the zip codes on her previous addresses. Those always seemed to be the first thing she forgot. But then...then the paperwork got hard.

"Tobe?" She wasn't sure exactly where he was. Hopefully he'd hear her.

"Yeah?" His voice was faint and distracted.

"Could you come here for a minute?"

"Just a sec."

She tapped her pen against the table while she waited and scanned the next page of the form. Oh hey, she knew that one. She filled in her salary and Toby's. She ought to know how much was in their savings account...but she always just left that to Toby. He cared more about it than she did.

"What's up?" Toby pulled out a chair.

June slid the sheet of paper over to him. "First, verify that the interests and hobbies I listed for you are the ones you want on here. And then there are some financial details that I should know but don't."

He scanned the sheet. "The interests are fine. You really don't know what's in savings?"

She shook her head.

He rolled his eyes and filled in that block as well as the one for the property value of their house. "I'll have to go look up the insurance information. Back in a minute."

At least he didn't know all the answers off the top of his head. She turned to the next page. Thankfully, they were both relatively healthy, so the serious medical conditions blocks needed only an 'N/A' before moving on. She filled in their educational background and flipped to the next sheet.

"Here we go." Toby came back holding a sticky note. He

took a few minutes to transfer the numbers onto the application form. "That it?"

"Ha. Not by a long shot. Ok, question one, what child would you like us to consider for your family. Include age, gender, physical and mental disabilities, ethnicities, et cetera." June looked at Toby.

He swallowed. "Um. You wanted an infant, right? So put infant...are you open to an older child or not really?"

Was she? She didn't want an insta-family. She wanted that whole newborn experience—she was already missing so much of what the average woman got to go through. Though her friends who'd been pregnant might say 'got to' was wrong, she'd never be able to know that for herself. "Not right now. Maybe later? I'm not ruling it out for down the road...we are going to do this more than once, right?"

Toby's eyebrows shot up. "I hadn't thought about it. But... yeah, most likely. We've always talked about having a big family. Even though we get to do it the hard way that hasn't changed for me."

June grinned. Her thoughts exactly. "Ok, so newborn. Ethnicities?"

He exhaled noisily.

"Yeah. That's kind of where I am. I mean, it's easy to put down Caucasian, obviously. But what else? I'm not opposed to other ethnicities, are you?"

He shook his head. "Maybe just don't list anything specific and we'll pray God brings us the right baby."

"So just healthy newborn?" June poised her pen over the paper.

"We can always change it later, right?"

Could they? "No idea. Though I guess we could turn down a placement, if it came to that." June cleared her throat. "Next, what kind of child do you not want us to consider?"

"Oh good grief. Really?" Toby angled his head to look at the paper. "Let's pray about it. Turn to the next page."

"It doesn't get any easier...though this one is at least a checklist." She held up the next page. "Mark the boxes next to your preferences. First up, gender."

"We're not specifying gender. You don't get to choose when you conceive, you shouldn't get to choose when you adopt."

June pursed her lips. That was reasonable. She made a checkmark beside 'Have no preference.' "Next up, a listing of possible ethnicities. Still good with everything?"

He nodded. "I think so. You?"

Did it matter that her child might not look like her and Toby? Not to her...would it matter to the child though? Was it fair to him, or her, to have parents of a completely different ethnicity? It might pose more challenges...but they'd get through it. "Yeah. Yeah, I'm still good. All right...I think I can do the rest for now. But we'll both have to go get physicals, and here's a sheet describing the autobiography you have to write."

Toby glanced down at the paper. "Seriously?"

She shrugged. "Apparently, yes. And this is all just the application. From what I've seen, the actual portfolio we put together is more in-depth."

"Great."

June chuckled. "I heard that sarcasm. Changing the topic slightly, though staying in the vein of somewhat painful activities...are we really going to Thanksgiving at my folk's? I need to let Mom know one way or the other."

"I really think we should. After last year...it'd be good for us to have a positive interaction with them. And I'd like to see my folks. I know we saw them over the summer, but..."

"Fair enough. Okay, I'll give her a call. And, on the positive side, we can tell them about adopting in person." For all the good that'd do.

31

"What happens now?" Lydia leaned across Kevin to reach one of the paper towel rolls positioned near the restaurant's eight flavors of barbecue sauce.

"Just push it closer to your side. We've got another down here." Toby nudged the towel holder toward the end of the table where the girls were sitting, elbowing Gareth in the process.

July used her fork to pry some chicken away from the bone. She dunked it in a pool of sauce. "They took the eggs into the lab and mixed them with Gareth's donation to the process. So we should have three embryos happily growing in little dishes. When they're big enough, I think they called them blastocysts? But honestly it's been so long since biology class I couldn't tell you anything more than that. I think it has to do with the number of cells? Anyway, they said Tuesday probably, they'll transfer them and then we wait to see if they implant."

"So right this very minute, you have three babies?" June grinned. "Congratulations, mama."

The blood drained from her face. Three more babies. She'd

already lost two. She'd likely lose at least one of these before the transfer. She forced the corners of her mouth up. "Thanks."

"I can't wait to hear how it goes. Kevin and I are just starting to talk about seeing someone—he's finally at a place where he's at least willing to talk about it...would you recommend Dr. DiCola?"

"Thanks, babe." Kevin sighed, shaking his head.

"What?" Lydia gestured to June and July. "This is what girls do. We happen to be girls. Just talk to Toby and Gareth and ignore us."

The men laughed and returned to the conversation about a new Xbox game.

"So, would you?"

June wrinkled her nose. "I'm probably not the best person to ask. My experience wasn't nearly as positive as July's has been. If I had to do it all over again...yeah, I'd probably go back. But if you do go see him, understand that you're not a person to him. You're just a piece of meat to boost his stats."

"I wouldn't go *that* far." July shook her head. "He definitely lacks bedside manner. I suspect that's owed, in large degree, to the fact that he's busy and successful at what he does. And he doesn't take questions very well, particularly if they're challenging his methods or what he thinks is best. But...his statistics are some of the best not only in the area, but the country."

"Hmm. I guess maybe I'll ask around a little more. If it was any other kind of doctor I might not care as much but when you're going to spend the majority of your time around them with no pants on...bedside manner is a little more important."

"Exactly!" June thumped the table. "That's it exactly. I hadn't really put my finger on why it bothered me so much. But that's it. I mean, other than my OB/GYN, who's a woman, mind you, I've been seen naked by exactly one other person and that's Toby. It's disconcerting—verging on humiliating—

to be naked from the waist down in front of scads of new people, especially when they can't even treat you like a person."

Lydia's smile didn't reach her eyes. "Less of an issue for me, but I get what you're saying. Did you research any of the other clinics in town?"

"I did some. But with your friend's recommendation...I just went with DiCola." June shrugged. "Sorry."

"I didn't do any research. I knew June had looked into it enough, so I just went with her recommendation. Gareth was okay with them, too, so they have an acceptable reputation in the medical community."

Lydia gnawed on a rib bone. "I always forget Gareth's a doctor. That makes me feel better."

July grinned. "He likes it when people forget he's a doctor. It keeps them from asking him to look at weird growths or rashes."

June snickered.

"Have you heard any more from Staci or Brad?" July leaned forward, her shirt hanging into the sauce on her plate. "Dang it."

Lydia shook her head. "Nope. I think she's talking with Maureen still, but I don't know. I knew Brad was a jerk, but I really never expected him to be so blasé about his wife having an abortion...I'm so glad that engagement ring he promised me never materialized. Anyway...got any great plans for Thanksgiving?"

JULY GROANED as she rolled to her side and curled into a ball. "They didn't say anything about it hurting like this."

Gareth rubbed her shoulders. "I'm sorry, babe. Can I get you anything? Maybe the heating pad?"

"Sure, let's try it." She winced as a knife stabbed through her abdomen and bile flowed up her throat. "Uuugh."

Gareth plugged in the heating pad and arranged it over her abdomen, tucking it in so it wouldn't slide off. He settled next to her on the bed with his tablet. "Hmm. I think maybe you ended up hyperstimulated. What you're describing in terms of pain location is consistent."

"Any recommendations for fixing it?" There had to be something. An epidural, maybe? She let out a measured breath. Or a bullet? Anything?

"Rest. Drink lots of water. Ibuprofin. Did you take any?" He set down the tablet.

"No...could you get me some? And some water?" The heat from the heating pad was slowly working its way into her abdomen, dulling the pain from stabbing to sharp throbs.

"'Course." He disappeared into the bathroom for a moment, returning with two caplets and a tall glass of water. "Let me help you sit up."

She downed the pills and water before easing back down. "Sorry to kill your plans for Saturday. If you want to go do something, you can. I'm just going to lie here and moan."

Gareth chuckled and rubbed her arm. "I didn't really have any plans. I'll hang here in case you need me. Maybe try to take a nap—sleep isn't going to hurt you."

July nodded, her eyes drifting shut.

A sharp twinge woke her. She rubbed her eyes and glanced at the clock. It was nearly noon. Gareth's side of the bed was cold, he must have wandered downstairs after she fell asleep. She didn't blame him, there wasn't much more boring than watching someone sleep. Unless you could fall asleep too. But Gareth had never been the world's best napper.

Her stomach growled. Definitely time to get up and find some food. Hopefully Gareth didn't already fend for himself. That would just solidify her uselessness as a wife.

She threw her legs over the side of the bed and stood. Her abdomen complained, but not as loudly as before her nap. Gritting her teeth she made her way downstairs.

Gareth looked away from the TV. "Feeling any better?"

"Some, yeah. You eat yet?"

"Not yet. Wanted to wait and see when you got up. Why don't you come sit and I'll go fix us something."

"I can do it." She shuffled toward the kitchen.

"Don't be silly." He patted the couch.

She pressed her hands into her stomach. It didn't stop the twinges, but it did reduce them some. "I got it. Thanks though. Grilled cheese?"

He gave a slow nod. "Sounds good."

32

June turned the page and scanned the information on the next sheet before flipping it as well. She continued thumbing through the pages and verifying information until she made it to the end of the small stack. "I think we're set. I'm glad you had the thought to ask about the doctor filling out the form based on our most recent physicals rather than having to wait six months before we could get another."

"I'm just glad they were okay doing it. Though I suppose we could have just paid out of pocket for another physical if they wouldn't. Just because insurance only allows one a year doesn't mean we can't do more than that if we have to." Toby slid the stack of papers in front of him and paged through them. "Looks good. Let's get it in the mail."

June slid the adoption forms into a manila envelope and sealed it. Her stomach twisted. It was only step one of a whole bunch of steps but still. It was progress. "I'll take it with me to work and put it in the outgoing box."

"Sounds good." Toby leaned forward and pressed his lips to hers. "Have a good day. I'll see you tonight."

She waved, grabbing the envelope off the counter along

with her purse and laptop bag. It was a later start than usual, but she'd wanted time to go over the final paperwork with Toby and get it ready to go. The sooner they had the initial application done, the sooner they could get their interviews started, put the portfolio together, and get a baby. So many steps still to take. Her heart sank. It seemed like the process was never ending. But others had gone through it successfully, so they would too.

Traffic was better than usual. Probably because it was so much later in the morning. It was almost enough to convince June to switch her schedule. But doing that would end any chance of taking lunch and seeing July. And even though things were sometimes strained between the two of them, she looked forward to that time each week. In fact...she punched in the speed dial for July on her phone.

"Hey, it's July. Leave a message."

June frowned. Why wasn't she answering? Maybe she was in a meeting? The voicemail beeped. "Hi, it's June. Lunch? I'm dropping our application in the mail today—seems like a reason to celebrate. Maybe we could get a dessert to share. Call me back."

Before long, she pulled into her parking spot. The building had switched to assigned spaces over the summer. At first, she'd hated it. Her assigned spot was on the second level, about as far from the elevator as you could get. But on days like today when she didn't beat the majority of the crowd in, having that spot sitting there empty was priceless.

When the garage elevator stopped in the main lobby, June detoured to the far side and down a short hall to the outgoing mail drop. Shooting up a brief prayer, she slid the envelope into the slot.

$\sim$

"Hey, I can't do lunch today, sorry."

June frowned and swiveled her office chair to look out the window. "Bummer. Tomorrow?"

"I'll be out tomorrow all day—it's transfer day tomorrow. That's why I can do lunch today, actually. I'm slammed and trying to get a little ahead so missing a day doesn't put me too far in the hole."

"All right. Well call me tomorrow and tell me how it went."

"Will do."

June clicked 'end' and stared out over the busy Arlington streets. It was good that they were both making headway. Even if this wasn't the way she'd planned to have a family, it wasn't second best. And if this was what God had for her and Toby, then she knew He'd make it beautiful somehow. Wouldn't He?

"May I speak to June please?"

"Speaking." June crossed the kitchen, dropping her laptop bag on the table, before heading upstairs, cell phone crunched between her shoulder and ear.

"Hi June, it's Faith from the adoption agency. I got your application packet today—you two were very quick." Humor laced her words.

"The mail was quick too, apparently. I just sent it yesterday. But, since we decided this is what we were doing, there didn't seem to be any reason to wait. That's okay...right?" June sat on the edge of the bed and pulled off her shoes, pausing to rub the aches out of the arches of each foot.

"Of course, of course. I was just surprised. I couldn't help but overhear a little of your discussion at break time and, well, I kind of figured you two would be spending several months figuring out your plan. That's typically what happens in situations where one person is thinking international adoption and the other domestic."

June chuckled. "I can imagine. But it was just a miscommunication. In this instance, easily remedied. What can I do for you? Did we forget something?"

"Oh, no. Everything looks great. I'm actually calling to see if we can set up your interviews. I'd like to start with interviewing you together here and then set up a different time to talk to each of you individually. I can combine that with coming by your house, if that's convenient? That gets my home visit taken care of as well."

"Sure, sounds good. Um, give me just a second to get back downstairs to the calendar, would you?"

"Of course."

June unbuttoned her slacks and shimmied out of them, draping them over the foot of the bed. She hurriedly tugged on pajama pants before skipping down the stairs to the kitchen where she and Toby kept a communal calendar. "Okay. When did you have in mind? During the week, evenings are best—though we're both generally off by four, four-thirty at the latest. So it wouldn't be too late."

Papers shuffling ruffled over the line. "What does Thursday look like for you? Maybe around five? Could you get to the office by then?"

Arlington to Fairfax at rush hour. It wouldn't be fun, but it was doable. "Sure. We can make that work."

"Great. I'll go ahead and get you set up. If you could bring your checkbook and the money orders for the state criminal background checks, that'd be great. The amounts are all in the paperwork folder. And if you have time to get your fingerprints done before Thursday, that'd help speed things along as well."

"Do we have the fingerprint cards? I didn't see those in the folder."

"Oh, that's right. No...you'll get those Thursday. So you can plan to have those done between your joint and individual interviews."

"Okay. Sounds good. See you Thursday."

June clicked off the phone and covered her mouth with her hands, breathing deeply. They were really doing this. She ran through the list of things that had to be accomplished before holding a baby in her arms. Her baby, not just a baby. If only every step was something she could control. But once they finished their home study and portfolio, it was all up to God. And a birth mother.

33

"It's so good to meet you again, one-on-one." Faith smiled and gestured to the couch.

June glanced around the room. It was the same one they'd attended the informational session in. It felt larger without so many people in it, but still cozy. She sat next to Toby and set her purse at her feet, digging around until she pulled out a notepad and pen.

Toby scooted back in his seat and leaned forward to rest his elbows on his knees. "Thanks for getting things rolling so quickly. We'd assumed we'd have to wait until after Thanksgiving...or even Christmas. This time of year always gets so busy."

"I try to keep that from happening. For so many, adoption is the next step after infertility and most couples are anxious to get a move on. I understand that. Especially when the wait, once all your ducks are in a row, can be a while. And that leads us into the first conversation I wanted to have. Why are you looking into adoption?" Faith crossed her legs and balanced a legal pad on one knee.

June glanced at Toby. He was looking at her. Did he want

her to lead off? He gave a small nod and encouraging smile. She cleared her throat. "We started trying to have a baby a little over a year ago. The shortened story is that I have PCOS, um polycystic ovarian syndrome, and don't ovulate. We worked with a reproductive endocrinologist earlier this fall and I don't respond to the medication. So the only thing really left is adoption."

"But it's not like we feel that it's a bad choice, or even a last resort." Toby frowned. "I've been kicking around the idea of adoption for a while. But I do think June—both of us, really— wanted to make sure we'd done everything we could medically before moving on."

Faith smiled. "That's fine. Everyone has a different journey when it comes to adopting. I'm not going to say one is better than the other. What matters to me is that you're not still actively pursuing treatment. Although it's allowed, I often find it causes difficulty in relationships to be doing both simultaneously so I discourage it. And I want to be sure that you're dealing with the grief of infertility. Do you think that you have closure there?"

Closure? Like 'it would just magically stop hurting' closure? June shook her head. "I...I'm not sure I'm ever going to get to a place where my infertility doesn't hurt. Does that pain control me? No. But...I'd say I'm still in the process of grieving. I don't know how long it's going to take...I didn't want to wait until I was completely over it to try to start moving on. Was that wrong?"

"I'm probably a little further along in that grief process—in some ways I think it's a tad easier for men. And, well, because I don't have a medical condition to go with it." Toby took June's hand and squeezed, offering an apologetic look. "But I also know that, for me at least, knowing that we've tried everything there is for us to try...that helps."

June nodded, waiting for his words to sting her heart. But there was nothing. Maybe she really was making progress in her grief. In some ways, it helped that he acknowledged that it was easier for him.

Faith wrote for a moment then looked up. "That all sounds perfectly normal. And no, I don't think you need to wait for some nebulous future time when there's no more grief before you adopt. In fact, I think sometimes the adoption process helps you move through your grief. It breaks you out of the depression and shuffles you into acceptance. You're making new plans, working on finding meaning in your journey. Just keep in mind that there are going to be times as you go through this that you'll be right back in anger or depression again. It's a cycle and everyone moves through it at their own pace. Also remember that you won't ever be the same person—or couple —you were before infertility."

That was true. June had already noticed changes. Little things—shifts in attitudes, an extra gentleness here or harshness there. Some of the shine had been rubbed off of them and their relationship, but it had left a patina of experience that she was learning to embrace.

Faith cleared her throat. "Tell me about filling out the application. Was it challenging for you to agree on ethnicity or medical conditions?"

Toby chuckled. "Surprisingly, no. Neither of us had any reservations about ethnicities. We live in a pretty diverse neighborhood, so there are kids of all nationalities out playing in the common areas. And while we don't know their parents very well at this point, we've never had any indication that it would be a challenge to get to know them. Our church is slightly less diverse, but they're a loving and open place—I can't see any major problems there, either."

"What about your families?" Faith scribbled a few notes.

June's heart plummeted into her stomach. There it was. She

glanced at Toby and pulled her lower lip between her teeth. "They're...going to have more reservations."

"Going to? Have you not talked to them about your plan to adopt yet?"

"We're going to next week. At Thanksgiving. We thought maybe talking to them in person would help." June wiggled. Why did she feel like a kid caught with her hand in the cookie jar?

"Hmm." Faith wrote some more. "And how will their reaction influence your decision to adopt?"

"It won't." Toby voice was flat. It only got that way when he was fighting anger. June rubbed her thumb over the top of his hand.

"He's right. It isn't going to make a difference. My parents are...set in their ways and very sure of themselves. We've done a number of things in our married life that they didn't agree with and, while it strains the relationship for a time, they generally come around." June blew out a breath. "Toby's parents will be on board. They considered adopting themselves, didn't they?"

He nodded. "Yeah, after I was born they had trouble conceiving. I even vaguely remember some of the conversations they had with me about it."

"Why didn't they pursue it?"

"Mom was pregnant with my sister and didn't know it." Toby chuckled. "She's been surprising them ever since."

Faith smiled at Toby before returning her gaze to June. "Do you think your parents will treat an adopted grandchild differently than a biological one?"

"No." June shook her head. They wouldn't, would they? "I honestly believe once they hold him or her for the first time, they'll forget all about adopted or biological. They're not bad people. They're just always right. I'm sure after a while, they'll be telling the story that adopting was their idea in the first place."

Toby snickered. "That would be just like them."

"And if they don't?" Faith raised her eyebrows.

"Then they'll miss out." June shrugged. She'd threatened to cut them out of her life before and meant it. She wouldn't have trouble doing it again if she had to. Hopefully it wouldn't come to that, but she'd protect her child at all costs.

Faith nodded and made a few notes. "All right. Let's shift gears some. Tell me how the two of you met."

"THAT WASN'T AS bad as I thought it was going to be." Toby snapped his seatbelt in place.

June nodded, her head relaxed against the headrest. It hadn't been bad, but it had still been exhausting.

"Hungry? We could hit a drive through. Or go nuts and find something a little nicer."

June's stomach churned. Despite her assurances to Faith, the upcoming conversation with her parents was already eating at her. It wasn't going to be pretty. Sure, they'd get through it. But that didn't mean it wasn't going to stink in the meantime. "Nah. Maybe just a soda? I'm...not really hungry."

Toby frowned. "You okay?"

"Yeah. Just thinking about my folks. And your folks. And next week...wondering if I can somehow engineer a work disaster that keeps me from being able to go home for the holiday after all."

He chuckled and patted her knee. "It's gonna be all right. I'm not looking forward to it either, but it'll be okay. And while I know you think my parents don't like you, you're wrong. And they'll at least be a respite from your parents flying off the handle about us adopting."

Yeah. That made it better. His parents were going to be the less stressful visit. She pressed her lips together and offered a weak smile. He wasn't wrong though. They would make it through. It helped that the two of them were on the same page. Her mom wouldn't be able to squeeze a wedge in to try and prove a point. And faced with a united front...Mom usually got it together and backed off. Eventually.

34

Gareth paced the back yard, a rake in his hand. It had only been five days—much too soon to know if implantation had occurred. The doctor didn't even want them to take a pregnancy test on their own. They had to wait eighteen days and go in for a blood test. Eighteen days. That put them firmly into December. The only positive to come out of it were travel and stress restrictions. July was supposed to avoid anything that would cause undue tension. And that firmly knocked out Thanksgiving with her family. And his. Though his parents hadn't invited them.

That wasn't a big surprise, though it still stung. He'd always assumed his family would stay close when he grew up, married, and started his own family. Now, with that family underway... there had to be some way to fix it. Didn't there? His parents had never been particularly close with his grandparents. Had they even visited every year? He shook his head, more like every other year, or every three years. He wanted more for his kids. Would his parents be willing to change? They were so determined not to meddle...but being a part of someone's life wasn't meddling. Why couldn't they see that?

"Hey." July wandered across the lawn, a glass of amber liquid in her hand. "I brought you out some tea. Though it doesn't look like you've actually done anything yet."

He smiled, reaching for the glass. "Thanks."

"You okay?"

"Mostly. Just thinking about the baby—babies—my parents, your parents...just family. I want our kids to know their grandparents. But I don't know how to make that happen with my folks."

"They'll come around when she's born, won't they?"

Gareth arched a brow. "She?"

July shrugged. "Didn't want to go with 'it.' Besides, with two of them in there, the odds are one of them's a girl, right?"

Technically, no. Each one had the same odds of being female—having two didn't make any change...but now probably wasn't the time for a lesson in probability. Particularly not when prob and stats nearly crushed their relationship in college. He cleared his throat. "Something like that."

She narrowed her eyes. "I can see what you're thinking. And no, contrary to your bizarre opinion, accountants don't actually need probability to do their jobs well. Sheesh. I get one C in a math class and suddenly I'm not fit for a career that uses math."

"I didn't say that." Gareth raised his hand to fend off the accusation.

"You thought it." July shook her head. "Anyway. I think your parents will come around. Have you...did you mention the procedure to them?"

"Not yet. I...wasn't sure how to bring it up. I figured maybe waiting until you were through the first trimester would be smarter this time anyway. And, really...do they need to know *how* you got pregnant?" They could just let people assume it had been natural, couldn't they?

She sighed. "I don't know. I guess as long as they don't run into June. Or my parents..."

"You're going to tell your parents?" He drained the last of the tea and leaned on the rake. "Really?"

"I feel like I have to. I mean..."

"How is it any of their business? You got pregnant and had a baby...what more do they really need to know? It's not as if we used someone else's eggs or sperm, where we'd potentially have to explain genetic differences." Gareth fumed. If she told her parents, they'd fuss about it. They fussed about everything that didn't fit into their perfect little box. Their daughters struggling with infertility was one of those things that definitely didn't fit into that box.

July puffed out her cheeks. "I'll think about it."

He frowned.

"It's not that I think you're wrong. You're not wrong. It's just that...I know how my family works. I've never yet successfully managed to hide something from my mom. And it's always worse when she finds out than if I just tell her about it before hand. Honestly, at this point she's going to be irritated that she didn't know before the procedure. Ostensibly because she would have wanted to pray, but realistically because she hates being left out."

Gareth scoffed. "Okay, I get that. But I still don't think we should tell her. You know how she feels about IVF. Even if you explain that we only created two embryos."

"Three."

"Fine, three. But one didn't even live a complete twenty-four hours. Does she really need to know about that one?"

July reached for his glass and shook an ice cube into her mouth, crunching it between her back teeth. "It's all or nothing with her. You know that."

How two normal—well, mostly normal—women like July and June had come from someone as bizarre as his mother-in-law was something Gareth was never going to understand. "Two, three. Doesn't matter. The fact that we only created what we were comfortable transferring isn't going to matter to her one bit. She'll launch into the lecture about playing God."

June closed her eyes. "I know. And that's why I've essentially lied about why we aren't coming for Thanksgiving and said you couldn't get away from work. Of course she then tried to get me to come without you, so I had to explain that it wasn't fair to leave you alone on Thanksgiving...honestly, it's just as well you didn't hear that whole conversation."

"I can imagine." The corners of his mouth twitched. He kissed her forehead. "Thanks for standing up for me. Look, for now, let's not say anything. If, once we announce the pregnancy, we want to get into details we can. But in the meantime, let's pray for wisdom on that."

"All right. I should probably put a bug in June's ear though. She's pretty good at keeping quiet when she knows she needs to. But if I don't explicitly tell her..."

"Go call her now." Gareth handed her the glass. "Thanks for the tea. Maybe another glass in, say, an hour?"

"Only if you've done some raking. I'll give you one freebie, but any more you have to earn."

Gareth laughed, a weight lifting from his shoulders.

"You're driving up tomorrow?" Gareth slid onto the stool next to Toby at the hip micro-brewery that took up a large storefront in the Ballston Mall.

"Yeah. Even though everyone is going to be leaving, we're hoping to get around some of the traffic by leaving early. Schools, I think, are half-day. So a lot of people won't be getting on the road until around one. By then we should be in Ohio, more than half-way to the western outskirts of Chicago."

"I guess you have to go up the day before since it's what, fourteen hours?"

"About that, yeah. Don't you remember our spring break road trips?" Toby grinned.

Gareth chuckled. He and Toby had taken several fun trips from Chicago during those weeks off in the spring. Since both had family nearby, there was less reason to head home during breaks—they saw their parents plenty. "Remember when we hit DC and they got that freak snow storm?"

Toby laughed. "We were very nearly late getting back. But that's the trip that convinced me this is where I wanted to job hunt when I graduated."

"And that's what pushed me to look out here as well. Even then, July wasn't willing to be too far from her sister."

"It's good I like you, man." Toby clapped Gareth on the back.

"Ditto." Gareth took a long drink of soda. "So, I know July talked to June, but I wanted to just mention it to you—just in case. We're not telling anyone about the IVF yet. Possibly not at all. Between July's mom and my family...we can't see how it's anyone's business. And frankly, I just don't feel like justifying our decision. You know?"

"Gotcha. Though I suspect with us dropping our adoption news there's not going to be a ton of room for letting something slip. But I'll try and make sure we don't say anything. When will you know if it worked?"

Gareth glanced at his watch to check the date. "Next Friday —December fifth. We've got a blood draw already scheduled for that morning. Though I suspect they'll do multiple checks to make sure the HCG is doubling like it's supposed to. Still, by then they ought to be able to say for sure that we're pregnant."

"Cool. Keep us posted."

"You know it. I suspect sometimes July calls June before she calls me when it comes to test results."

Toby grinned. "I don't imagine you're wrong. It does, at least, work both ways."

"Hey. Do you think you could grab a pizza on your way out of town and bring it back? I've been craving Giordano's."

"You sure it's July who's pregnant?" Toby laughed when Gareth punched his shoulder. "Yeah, I can do that. But you have to share. I know June and I'll hit 'em up at least once while we're there, but really, can you have too much stuffed pizza?"

"Not to my knowledge, no." Gareth cleared his throat. "Did you and June have any problems agreeing to adopt?"

Toby's brows shot up. "No. Why?"

Gareth frowned. "I just...July's really opposed and I was wondering if it was a family thing. I mean, I gather that Mom and Dad aren't big fans so...how'd June get to be open to it?"

"Not sure. She's never been against it that I know of. I'll ask her."

Gareth nodded. So much for that. He'd been hoping for some ammunition, something that would help him convince July to give it more than a passing thought. Even though their insurance had covered the bulk of the treatment, IVF wasn't a particularly fiscally viable way to continue to expand their family. Not with all the risk and possibilities for failure.

35

June set the pile of plates in the sink. It was odd being back home for Thanksgiving. Usually her mom and dad travelled to them, or they skipped getting together. She couldn't say why, but she hadn't been back to the outskirts of Chicago since she and Toby married. Nothing had changed. Mom wasn't known for redecorating, but she'd been married and out of the house long enough that it was odd to find her bedroom still set up as if she'd be home from college at any moment. Maybe she should offer to take the rest of her things with her when she left. Or would that upset her mother? Did she like having those reminders around?

She pulled open the dishwasher. Empty. At least Mom hadn't used the extra-fancy china that had to be washed by hand. She turned on the faucet and rinsed the plates before loading them into the bottom rack.

"You didn't have to do that, dear." Betty came into the kitchen with another pile of dishes.

"I know, but it's just as easy to load them as it is to dump them in the sink."

Betty chuckled. "I'm glad some of my training rubbed off."

June followed her Mom's gaze to the dishwasher rack. "Did I do it wrong?"

"No. Sorry, habit. Your father still can't seem to get it right, despite having been married almost forty years. With the same dishwasher for the last fifteen of those."

June smiled. Her dad most likely messed it up on purpose as a way to get under her mom's skin. He enjoyed poking at her more annoying buttons. When June was a teenager and having one of those typical mother-daughter arguments about nothing, he'd told June he kept hoping Betty would see the absurdity of her behavior if he just teased her enough. Didn't look like that tactic was working yet. But it was so much a part of their relationship...neither one would know what to do if he quit.

"Will you bring the pumpkin pie to the dining room when you come? It's in the fridge. There's whipped cream next to it as well."

June watched her mother hurry from the room. Probably loathe to leave Toby alone with Dad, since Dad just let Toby hang out like a member of the family and Mom always had to act the hostess. At some point she'd get used to the idea that they were married. Or at least, that's what June kept telling Toby. He never seemed to believe her. She wasn't sure she believed it either. She rinsed her hands before grabbing the dessert.

"This pie looks wonderful, Mom." June set it down in front of her dad, along with the whipped cream, a knife, cake server, and spoon. "Do we need plates, too?"

"I stacked them on the buffet behind Toby." Betty pointed to the antique cherry buffet that stood sentry in the precise center of the dining room wall.

"Got 'em." Toby snaked an arm over the top of his chair and grabbed the plates.

June sat and passed them to her dad. "Thanks, sweetie."

"I'm assuming everyone wants some? Your mother does make an amazing pie. It was her French silk pie that won my heart."

"Oh, stop." Pink stole across Betty's cheeks and she slapped playfully at Ed's arm.

Ed leaned over and kissed Betty on the lips. "Make it again and I'll show my appreciation."

June caught Toby's veiled gagging motion out of the corner of her eye and fought a grin. It had grossed her out as a teen, but now she found her parent's open affection adorable. Hopefully she and Toby would be embarrassing their children when they were older as well.

Ed winked at June and sliced into the pie. He slid a hearty piece onto a plate and dropped a generous scoop of whipped cream on top. "Pass that on down to Toby. You want about the same?"

Her mouth watered as she handed the pie to Toby but she shook her head. "Maybe half that, or slightly less than half that, even."

Betty's face visibly relaxed. Ed frowned. "That's hardly enough to even get a taste. It's Thanksgiving."

He cut another large slice and covered it in whipped cream. "Here now. And you." He turned to Betty and fixed her with a stern gaze. "Leave her be. She's gorgeous, as she's always been. As all three of my girls are. Don't you think, Toby?"

Toby slipped his arm around June's shoulders. "Always have. Always will."

Betty's mouth was pinched. "Well don't give me that much. Some of us have to watch our figures."

June looked over at Toby, then back at her pie. How did her mom manage to ruin any possible enjoyment of a sweet treat with one simple phrase? She pushed the whipped cream off to the side and cut a thin sliver down one side of the slice of pie. She'd just eat that, give the rest to Toby.

"So." June took a tiny bite, closing her eyes as rich pumpkin exploded on her taste buds. "Mm. This is great, Mom."

"Thank you, dear." Betty poked at her slice of pie, taking up a teeny bite.

June looked at Toby. He gestured for her to go on. She cleared her throat and started again. "One of the reasons we decided to make the trip out this year is that Toby and I have some news."

A grin split across Betty's face. "You're pregnant! Oh honey, that's so wonderful. Isn't it great, Ed?"

"No. Mom." June held up her hand. "Let me finish. I'm not pregnant—we've decided to adopt."

Silence fell over the room.

Ed cleared his throat. "Well. That's...nice. When...or...well, how does that work?"

"Who cares how it works?" Betty dropped her fork on her plate with a clatter. "What on earth put this ridiculous idea in your head?"

Toby laid his hand on June's arm. "Mom. It's not ridiculous. June and I want a family. We're unable to do that biologically. So we're going to adopt."

Betty frowned. "Whose fault is it?"

"What do you mean, fault?" June crossed her arms.

"He said you can't have biological children. Surely you're not both defective. So whose fault is it? It's a simple question."

"Betty...that's uncalled for." Ed frowned and pushed his slice of pie away from his place at the table.

June leapt to her feet, her chair flipping over with a bang as it smacked the floor. "No, Dad, it's fine. You want to know whose fault it is? It's mine. I'm broken. The same thing that's caused all this weight gain has also rendered my ovaries useless lumps of tissue that don't do what God intended them to do. So get off your high horse, Mom. 'Cause the genes that suck? They're half yours."

JUNE LOOKED up at the light tap on the door. "Yeah?"

Toby slipped into the room, closing the door and leaning against it. "What is it with your family and Thanksgiving?"

She managed a weak chuckle. "I think it's just me. I bring out the turkey in everyone."

Toby groaned and crossed to sit next to her on the bed. "For what it's worth, your dad lit into your mom pretty badly."

Her shoulders fell. She didn't want to cause trouble between her parents, even if a small sliver of warmth wormed into her heart that her dad would stand up for her. "Now I'll have to fix that, too."

"No." He rubbed her leg. "No, I don't think you will. Your mom is...unhappy that you haven't come out of your room. I told her not to come check on you, figured you needed a little space. But I think she understands she crossed a line."

"That's great. But do you think there'll ever be a time when she can figure that out *before* crossing the line? I'm so tired of always having to be the one who overlooks her comments. And really, Toby...how can we inflict her on a child? Maybe we just need to decide our kids are going to grow up with only one set of grandparents."

"June." Toby shook his head. "You don't mean that. Don't say it just to make a point. I understand what you're getting at but...don't make things worse."

It didn't help that he was right. Wasn't her mother ever going to have to pay the price for her rash words? She sighed. "Fine."

Toby kissed the top of her head. "Ready to come back out? I saved your pie."

JUNE SLOUCHED against Toby in the living room. Ed had turned on a football game when Betty had gone to lie down and then promptly buried his nose in a book. June stared at the TV. Why did people enjoy this?

Toby groaned. "Flag on the play. Where's the flag?"

She blew out a breath. At least someone was enjoying themselves. "Whatcha reading, Dad?"

Ed flipped the spine of the book up so she could see. "It's a Christian thriller. Engrossing, really, and on the creepy side, too."

June studied the cover. A pawn was flopped over in a pool of...was that blood? "So not, in fact, about chess?"

"Ha. No." He lay the book in his lap, his thumb holding his place. "Your mother loves you, you know that, right?"

"Yeah. I know. She has an odd way of showing it a lot of the time, but still I know it." June sighed. "I'd hoped that the excitement of knowing a grandchild was on the way might be enough to get over her objections to us adopting. Though I guess she didn't actually object to the adoption, just to me being genetically deficient and useless."

"Hey now." Toby looked away from the TV. "No one said you were either of those things. Not even your mother."

No one said it. They didn't have to. The whole concept of fault made it clear. God made her broken. She'd almost come to terms with that, though she still didn't understand why. Did her mother really need to rub her face in it?

"Toby's right. Neither of us think you're broken. What your mother was asking, in a completely wrong and terrible way, was if there was anything medically you could try?"

June shook her head. "We tried. I don't respond to the medications. The doctor said he'd done everything he could. But I never figured Mom would be okay with any sort of assisted reproduction."

Ed shrugged. "She's growing. We have several young families at our church who have used in-vitro to get pregnant. And while she still has some concerns about it, she's starting to understand that it's one way God can choose to give couples children."

June filed that away. Maybe July would have an easier time talking to their parents than she'd expected. "And adoption is another."

"We know. And if that's the route you're feeling led to explore, we're going to support you, one hundred percent."

36

June tipped the seat back and stretched out her legs. They were just entering Maryland—only a few hours left and they'd be home. The rest of the trip had gone reasonably well. Her mother, at least, had stopped being obnoxious. So...progress.

"I can still smell the pizza." Toby glanced over with a grin.

"Me too. It's been making me hungry for the entire drive. Think Gareth would notice a missing piece?"

"Probably. We could dig into ours." Toby licked his lips.

"Thought about that. Then tried to figure out how you eat stuffed pizza while doing anything else. I always manage to spill sauce on my shirt even when I'm sitting at a table."

Toby wrinkled his nose. "Oh, sure. Be logical."

"I have my moments." June glanced over her shoulder and shook her head. "Those moments did not occur while shopping with your mother."

He laughed. "I wasn't going to say anything. What all did you get?"

"Practically everything a nursery needs for the first year. Your mom got a little over excited." It had been contagious.

June smiled thinking of their marathon trip through the aisles of Babies 'R Us and two smaller, local boutiques.

Gareth frowned. "What if you got the gender wrong?"

"Oh, it's all reasonably gender neutral. And we didn't get much in terms of clothes—your mom said it's better to wait until the baby's born for a lot of clothing choices because you never know how large they're going to be. She said when you were born she had a whole wardrobe in the tiniest size that she had to give away since she'd clipped off all the tags and washed them in anticipation."

He chuckled. "Ten-pound babies will do that for you. But it's a good point."

"So we only got a few little sleepers—and not newborn size, the zero to three month size. Everything else is either baby gear, toys, or decorative."

Toby's eyes flicked to the rear view mirror. "How big does she think our guest room slash soon-to-be nursery is?"

June shrugged. "It all fit in the car."

"Was that the rubric you used? Will it fit in the car?"

"Pretty much, yeah. After my mom's reaction, it was just nice to have someone be unashamedly excited about the prospect of a grandchild, without any care or concern for where the baby came from or whose fault it was there'd be no shared genetics." Whatever reservations she'd had before about her in-laws had dissipated on this trip. Her mother-in-law, in particular, was a gem.

"Fair enough." He snapped his mouth shut and took a deep breath, expelling it slowly. "I'm sorry about your mom. Though you've got to admit she got better by the time we left."

"Please don't be sorry. *I'm* the one who's sorry."

"Hey, for all their faults, they created you. And you're pretty great."

June grinned and slipped her hand in his. "Thanks."

"HERE YOU GO." Toby set a steaming slice of pizza down on the table in front of June. "What are you working on?"

June looked up from her laptop. "Making a few photo collages to use in our parent profile. I want to have it ready to give to Faith when we have our individual interviews on Friday. I was hoping maybe you could meet me at the police station right near the Court House Metro sometime before then. They do fingerprinting."

"Sure. I suspect tomorrow will be busy getting caught up after the holiday—you know how clients are. Maybe Tuesday?"

"That'll work. I'm thinking Bob'll have at least one, possibly two, big meetings tomorrow. He's panicked about something but, so far, hasn't been willing to say what. I haven't pushed much though. After last fall...I'm keeping my head down and enjoying being a team lead with a team who gets their work done and doesn't cause drama."

Toby chuckled. "Besides fingerprints and the parent profile, what's left for us to do?"

"Just the interviews. Then once the background checks come in, Faith writes up a report and our home study is done. At that point...we just wait."

"And pray."

June nodded. "Probably a lot of both. Here." She swiveled the computer so he could see the screen. "What do you think of this?"

Toby cocked his head. "I like it. It's a nice overview of our wedding—plus it shows how big our extended families are."

"And that we can get together and still smile. At least for special occasions. Okay. I want to have ten or so pages like this. I was thinking our wedding, which is this one. Then the house and yard. Maybe immediate family? You know how we hang out with July and Gar, and we see my parents pretty frequently, plus a photo from this weekend to show your family?"

He nodded. "That sounds good. What else."

"I was hoping you might have some ideas. I know we can't leave it at just three pages, but frankly...I'm stuck." What would push them over the edge in a birthmother's mind? Their 'Dear Birthmother' letter was good. But pictures...in today's world, pictures were going to push it over the edge.

"What about kind of a day-in-the-life thing? We could take a picture of us all dressed up for work with our laptop bags, maybe our offices, dinner together, and then kicked back playing cards or something?"

June scoffed. "We haven't played cards in ages."

"Yeah, but we used to. And I'd like to start again...plus a picture of us watching TV doesn't seem as inviting."

The meager direction they'd been given did say to emphasize the fun and interactive parts of life. "Okay. That's four. Only six more ideas."

He laughed. "Same vein—typical Saturday?"

She drummed her fingers on the keyboard. "Maybe include a hike? I think we have some pictures from that time we went hiking at Great Falls. We might have to stage some of the other stuff though. That could work. Five more."

"Nuh-uh. Your turn now." Toby cut off a piece of his pizza.

June pushed the laptop toward the center of the table and cut into her own slice. "Mmm. Why can't someone out here figure out Chicago-style pizza? *Real* Chicago-style pizza, not Uno's."

"No idea, but it's a tragedy."

They ate in silence for several minutes. Ideas flitted in and out of June's head. How did you stick to the truth of who you were but still make it interesting? What kinds of photos made you look like a couple who'd be great parents?

"What about that vacation we took to Niagara Falls?"

Toby frowned. "What about it?"

"Well, we both said we like to travel...maybe it'd be good to show that we have done a little bit of it. It's not all pipe dreams."

"Sure. Maybe that could even be two pages. One for Niagara and another on our cruise."

"Hmm. I hadn't thought of doing two page spreads. I could probably do two pages on the house—it'd give more detail. So what are we up to now, eight?"

"Yeah."

Was that enough? June finished the pizza and wiped her fingers on her napkin. She carried her plate to the sink and set it down. "Maybe that's enough. It's certainly a place to start. Keep thinking though and let me know if you come up with more. I'll get started on these."

37

July jumped up from her seat in the crowded sandwich shop and threw her arms around June. "Gosh I missed you."

June laughed. "Feels like it's been more than a week, doesn't it? How was your Thanksgiving?"

Boring? Stressful? Nerve wracking? July discarded the words as they popped into her head. "Quiet. We should've taken the pastor up on his invitation, but it didn't feel right to horn in on their family celebration. Particularly not once Lydia let it slip that it was the first time all of her sisters were going to be home in a handful of years."

"Quiet's good though, right?" June unwrapped her sandwich and took a bite.

July opened the container on the salad she'd ordered. "You'd think so. But it gives you entirely too much time to obsess. Every little twinge or tickle...you feel them. And I'm trying so hard to do what the doctor said and not take a home test. I have a box of them calling to me from under the bathroom sink though, which makes it harder."

"Why not just take one with the understanding that a negative might just mean it's too early?"

July sighed. How many times had she had this argument with herself over the last four days? "You're as bad as Gareth. I don't think I need to get on that emotional rollercoaster. I couldn't take it."

June wiped the corners of her mouth. "I guess I can see that. Sort of a Catch-22, isn't it?"

"Exactly. I did, at least, think to bring some work home with me. So that helped. But...five more days. How am I going to make it to Friday?"

"Four and a half, it's lunchtime." June smiled over the top of her soda.

"Fine. The question remains." July stabbed at her salad. It was absolutely unappetizing. Was the lettuce bad? The smell turned her stomach. She pushed it away. "Anyway...how are Mom and Dad? You didn't call screaming or sobbing...I took that as a good sign."

June snickered and relayed the initial conversation about adopting and her father's explanation from later. "So really, you're going to have a much easier time if you decide to share about your IVF. 'Cause Mom and Dad appear to be completely on board with that. They just took some persuading to be okay with adopting."

"I'm sorry. That sounds...not fun." And no matter what Mom was saying now, it was likely to come up again and be just as ugly. July's own thoughts on adoption were definitely influenced by the negative vibe her mother always gave off whenever the topic arose. It couldn't possibly be completely gone, could it? She'd cross her fingers that, if nothing else, June's baby never had to know how less-than-supportive one set of grandparents had been. "How were Toby's folks?"

A grin spread across June's face, lighting up her features. "They were awesome. I think, for the first time ever, I finally caught a glimmer of what Toby's been trying to tell me about his family. His mom was so excited about us adopting that she dragged me out shopping. I'm not even sure I'll need a baby shower—she went a little crazy."

"Well, if you get extras of things, maybe you'll be able to share with me." July winked.

"Friday, huh?"

"Yeah." July clasped her fingers together. "If this works...are you going to be upset?"

June pursed her lips and was silent for several heartbeats. "You know...I don't think I am. I can't say I'm thrilled that the possibility of biological children is completely gone for me and Toby. But I can say that adoption feels right. There's peace... maybe it's slightly uneasy at times, when I think of what could have been—what I feel *should* have been—but I'm not as hung up on that as I used to be."

July watched her sister and nodded slowly. June did look more relaxed than she'd been in a long time. Some of that might be coming from four-days away—though visiting Mom and Dad only barely qualified as a vacation. The rest...maybe it was peace. Would she ever get to the point where she saw that in her own mirror in the morning?

"GARETH, can you come look at these with me?"

After a minute, Gareth came into the office, a bowl of ice cream in one hand and a glass of milk in the other. He hooked his chair with one foot and rolled it over to July's desk. "What are we looking at?"

July eyed his ice cream. "That for me?"

"It can be. You want it?" He held out the bowl.

Her mouth watered. She'd picked up a gallon of cookie dough ice cream on her way home. It wasn't a craving, per se, but she'd been thinking about it the whole afternoon. Still...she didn't *need* ice cream. "No. Well, maybe a bite?"

Gareth shook his head and set the bowl on the corner of her desk. "Now we can both reach it. So...what's this?"

July scrolled down a little so the whole image fit on the screen. "June sent over the photo pages she and Toby want to use in their parent profile for us to look at. I'm not sure if we're supposed to just say it's great or really scrutinize to try and find something wrong...but I figured two sets of eyes are better than one."

"Works for me. I like this one." He pointed to one of the images in the collage. "That's always been one of my favorite pictures of us."

"Yeah. Their wedding was a lot of fun. I'm still glad we decided not to do a double wedding. I imagine Mom and Dad would have preferred for us to just have one from a cost stand-point. Especially since there was so much overlap in attendance."

Gareth shrugged. "Knowing your mom, if she really preferred that, that's what we would've done."

She chuckled. "All right, that's fair. Here's the next one."

They spent about a half an hour looking through the eight photo pages, reminiscing about the times they'd shared with June and Toby during the events pictured.

"That was fun. And I think a great snapshot of them as a couple and their life together so far."

July nodded. "Agreed. I'll let her know she's done well. I hope it works for them. Quickly."

Gareth rubbed her shoulder.

"What?"

He opened his mouth, snapped it shut and shook his head. "Never mind."

"No. What?" July crossed her arms.

"It's just...I know you're still on the fence about adopting, but doesn't it help, just a little, to see what needs to be done? I would think it would demystify the process a little."

Demystify? She hadn't been mystified. Throwing some scrapbook pages together wasn't the problem. Nor was the paperwork—she could do forms; she was an accountant after all. But what did you do after all the paperwork was finished? You waited. With no idea how long that was going to take. You just had to hope that something you did in those pages or your letters hit just the right tone with a birthmother and birthfather. But how did you know? Maybe there weren't people out there looking to place a baby with an accountant and medical researcher. Neither of those were glamorous jobs. What did they have to recommend themselves to anyone? Nothing that would show up in a what, fifteen page—max—portfolio.

"I guess we'll see. Right now, I just want it work for June."

38

Toby flipped through one of the five copies of their portfolio sitting on the table. June had done a great job. They were professional looking, but still gave off the casual coziness that he'd always associated with them as a couple. The formal portrait on the front cover was one of his favorites. They'd had it taken last year at Christmas as part of their gifts for both sets of parents. Rather than opting for a studio, they'd found a freelance photographer and gone to Mount Vernon for their candlelight tour. They'd found a spot near one of the brick outbuildings with candles flickering in the windows, a light dusting of snow, and some kind of wreath —was it holly? The result was charming.

He read through the letter to the birth parents again and blinked to clear excess water from his eyes. June had a way with words when she wanted to. It was open and heartfelt. And she'd captured him, as well. He was in every part of the letter— it wasn't just all her with his name tacked on at the end. It wasn't as if he hadn't helped. Just not perhaps as much as he should have. Of course, she hadn't really asked him to.

Toby flipped to the photos and smiled. The collages had turned out well. They hadn't come up with any other ideas, but the eight pages really showcased them and everything they were, both together and individually. Would it be enough to convince someone to choose them? No way to know, really. But there was nothing more they could do that would make it any better. Hopefully it was like Faith had said at their initial meeting—there's a shoe for every foot. You just have to get enough people to try it on to find the match. That was the part that would take time.

"What do you think?" June wrapped her arms around him from behind and peeked around his right shoulder.

"They're great." Toby kissed the top of her head. "I was just thinking that there's really no way we could improve them."

She beamed. "I'm glad you think so. I was pretty pleased with how they turned out. And if nothing else, we know we've done our best—given a clear representation of who we are. If that's not a match with people, well, that's okay."

"When is Faith coming?" He glanced at the clock on the stove. It was just after four.

"She should be here any minute. I imagine it might take a tad longer than she expected—Friday traffic and all." The doorbell chimed. June chuckled. "Or not."

Toby turned, watching as June opened the door and welcomed the social worker. He lifted a hand in greeting as Faith made her way into the kitchen.

"Toby. It's great to see you. Getting cold out there—it's almost starting to feel like winter."

He laughed. "It is December. Though around here you never know. Can I take your coat?"

Faith shrugged out of her coat and held it out. Toby took it to the dining room and draped it over the back of a chair. When he got back to the kitchen, June was giving Faith a glass of water and showing her the portfolios.

"These look great. Nice job." Faith tucked them into the large bag she had slung over her shoulder. "I'll get them into circulation as soon as I've got the final home study approvals. It'll likely be a week, maybe two, before your child protective services clearance and criminal background checks come back. But once we're finished with the individual interviews today, I can write up the majority of my report so it's just a matter of including the final clearances when they come."

"That's great." Toby rubbed his hands together. "I'm looking forward to having this step out of the way."

June shrugged. "At least this is an active step. Once it's done, we just wait. Right?"

Faith nodded. "Basically, yes. But there are some books and classes I'll recommend that will help eat up some of that waiting time. Now, who wants to go first?"

"Ladies first?"

June shook her head, pressing a hand to her stomach. "Um. Why don't you go first? I'll be back down in a bit."

Toby raised his eyebrows. "You okay?"

June nodded from the doorway. "Yeah. Of course."

He frowned, watching her leave then turned to Faith. "Well, I guess I'm up. Why don't we sit in the living room?"

When they were settled, Faith balanced a legal pad on her crossed legs. How did she manage that? He'd tried it after their joint interview, simply because she'd made it look so easy. He'd gotten the notepad to stay, finally, but whenever he tried to write, he'd had to twist himself into a bizarre contortion. Even then it wasn't legible.

"These interviews don't take long. And when we're done, I'd like a brief tour of your house. I'm just checking that you have smoke detectors and room for a baby, that kind of thing." Faith's smile was calm and reassuring.

"Okay. I'm pretty sure June mentioned that was on the slate for today, but I'll admit I wasn't paying a ton of attention. She caught me while I was trying to check the score of a game. My dad and I have a difference of opinion on a few key quarterbacks—it tends to get a little heated during fantasy football time." Toby grinned.

"Ah. My husband's a big fantasy football man. I'll admit I don't see the appeal—but I do spend quite a bit of time watching HGTV and I think he'd say the same about my favorite shows."

Toby chuckled. "You should meet my brother-in-law. He has this whole fantasy home builder game spec'd out in his mind. I don't think it'll ever catch on, but maybe I'm wrong."

"See now, that sounds interesting to me. Definitely let me know if he ever tries to get it up and running. Now, so we don't end up making June any more nervous than she is by taking too long, let's jump in." Faith cleared her throat. "How have you found the application process?"

Toby shrugged. "Pretty straightforward, really. And...June's been doing the bulk of it, giving me assignments for the pieces I need to do. But any of the combined parts she's put together and then I've looked them over. I made a few tweaks here and there but she did a good job. Once she throws herself into something, she does it full throttle."

"Does that ever cause problems in your marriage?"

"Sure, sometimes. But it's something I've known about her since we met, so I can usually roll with it. Even though she can get wrapped up in things, and I tend to take a slower, wait and see approach. I think really we just balance each other out. You know?"

Faith scribbled on her note pad, nodding. "Do you fight?"

"Is there a married couple who doesn't?" Toby scratched his nose. "We do—they're not screaming fits or anything—but they're definitely disagreements. Usually we hash it out right away, but sometimes we'll call time and take an hour or so to calm down, get to a place where we can talk it out rationally. I can only think of one big fight that we've had, and even that got worked out eventually."

"What would you do if you couldn't work through it on your own?" Faith set her pen down, her eyes meeting his.

"Go see the pastor, most likely. I think we both respect him —he's the reason we go to our church—and having seen him in action with some friends...I think he'd be the first place to start." It probably wasn't necessary to mention that the friends were July and Gareth. They were friends, even if they were also related.

"Have you given any thought to how, if you adopt a child who's different ethnically from you, you'll incorporate their ethnic heritage into their upbringing?"

Toby blinked. What did that mean? They were adopting domestically—didn't that mean the babies were Americans, first and foremost? He frowned. "Not much, actually. I guess... maybe I don't understand how important that is."

Faith shifted. "It's important that children—particularly when they look different from their parents—have interactions with people of their own ethnicity. That helps them understand those differences."

Oh. Was that all? "We have a fairly multi-cultural neighborhood, and sphere of acquaintances. I don't think any child we adopt would ever feel like they stuck out based on their skin color."

"Hm." Faith scribbled some more on her notepad. "I'll circle two of the books on the list I'm leaving today—you really need to prioritize those, try to read them as soon as you can."

Toby's heart sank. Had he just botched the interview because he didn't see the need to point out ethnic differences to his kids? Wasn't the whole idea behind ending discrimination to raise kids not to notice them?

Faith moved on to ask about his childhood and family. Those questions, at least, he could answer. All in all, it wasn't a terrible process. Other than botching the ethnicity thing.

"Hey, June?" Toby hollered up the stairs. "Your turn."

39

As June passed Toby on the stairs she whispered, "How was it?"

Toby shrugged, whispering back, "Good. Mostly. House tour when you're done."

She frowned, watching him take the stairs two at a time. What did he mean by 'mostly'? She took a deep breath and pasted on a bright smile. "Hi. Sorry about that—my stomach got all twisted up and I realized I needed to lie down for a minute."

Faith chuckled. "Not a problem. It's normal to be nervous, but I promise, there aren't right or wrong answers here. I just want to get a feel for how you two work as a couple and what your parenting is likely to look like."

That was doable. And she and Toby had talked about it enough that their answers shouldn't be too different. That was probably important. Too bad they hadn't known exactly what to expect ahead of time though, they could've ensured they had everything straight. What was wrong with her? They didn't need to get their stories straight—it wasn't as if they'd committed a crime and were trying to keep from being arrested.

"So to start off, tell me a little about your family. How you grew up, what your parents are like, that sort of thing." Faith folded her hands on top of her legal pad and smiled.

Oh great, starting off with the fun topic. June chuckled. "My family is loud. I think that's probably the best word to describe them. Mom in particular, though my twin sister July can hold her own. And she has the red hair to prove it. Dad's a little calmer most of the time, but if he gets riled up, watch out. I tend to be a bit quieter, but I can wade in if I need to. Still, we had a great childhood—lots of love and laughing, solid Christian values, and I don't remember ever worrying that my family would fall apart. My parents are still married—and happy about it."

"Would you say you and Toby are loud as well?"

June shook her head. "Definitely not. Though we can both be loud if needed, I think we both make a concerted effort not to default to that. Neither of us is particularly keen on yelling as a form of communication. We try to talk things out, and if we can't, we take a break until we're calmer."

Faith wrote on her pad for a minute then looked up. "What are you planning to do about discipline for your children?"

Did she dare mention that she wasn't diametrically opposed to spanking? She cleared her throat. "I think you have to figure out what works for the child. Not everyone is going to respond to the same kinds of discipline. I also think, though, that you start gentle—redirection when they're younger, time-out, that kind of thing. I'm not one-hundred-percent sure that I could ever bring myself to spank, but if the situation warranted it, I wouldn't be opposed to it. I think the one thing that's a must though is that you don't do it in anger."

The questions continued, skipping here and there between marriage and parenting and her own upbringing. June didn't see any type of rhyme or reason, though maybe the point was to keep her honest by virtue of being unpredictable? Either way, she wasn't finding any of them hard to answer.

"I saw that you and Toby haven't specified any particular ethnicities that you're interested in adopting. If you're matched with a child of a different ethnicity, how do you plan to incorporate their ethnic heritage into their upbringing?"

June frowned. "I...I'm not sure I understand what you're asking. I suppose if we were adopting from Korea or somewhere in Africa, I could see that it would be important to help them understand their birth culture. But we're in the domestic program, right? So their ethnic heritage—their birth culture—it's American, isn't it?"

Faith shook her head. "Think about the African Americans you know, or the Hispanics. Is how they live different from you? Are those things your child should have in their life, even if their parents don't share their ethnicity?"

June pulled her bottom lip between her teeth. She knew, in passing, a few Hispanic families. Did they speak Spanish in the home? Maybe to the grandparents. They did tend to have multiple generations living together...but she wasn't going to invite her parents to move in simply to provide that experience. "I guess that's something we'll have to think more about—maybe do some research. Do you have any books you can recommend?"

Faith chuckled. "I'll leave a list with you." She glanced down at her notepad, wrote another line then capped her pen. "Okay. I think that pretty much wraps it up. Now I just need a quick tour of your beautiful home and I'll be out of your hair so you can get on with your Friday night."

JUNE SHUT the door and turned the key in the deadbolt before looking at Toby. "Well. I bombed one of the questions. But otherwise I think I did all right."

Toby held out his arms, wrapping them around her when she stepped in. "I'm pretty sure I missed at least one. What'd you have trouble with?"

"Something about their ethnic identity."

Toby began to laugh.

"What?" She tilted her head up so she could see his face.

"That's the one I couldn't answer. I did, at least, manage not to say exactly what I was thinking. So that's something."

June cleared her throat. "You did better than me then. I... basically said I thought it was a stupid question."

"All I could think of were stereotypes of various ethnicities. Did she want us to say we'd encourage an African American child to listen to rap and belt his pants below his knees? I mean...what are we supposed to do?" Toby gave her a tight squeeze and released her.

"I guess just provide opportunities to be around other kids who look like them. But they're going to get that in this area anyway." June sighed. "I don't know. I guess we'll figure it out from the books on the list she left us."

"Assuming we didn't disqualify ourselves with our ignorance."

June fwapped his arm. "Don't be a negative Nelly. She said she was going to get busy typing up our report. She took our portfolios and fingerprint cards. I think we're okay."

"Okay. You're right. I just felt so bad when she gave me that look after I, essentially, couldn't answer the question. I figured I'd just killed our chances. I could just hear your mom." His voice went up an octave and took on a whine. "So it's June's fault you can't have biological children and Toby's fault you can't adopt. It's a match made in heaven."

Laughing, June shook her head. His impression of her mom

was getting better, though it still tended toward the Monty Python-esque old lady once he got going. "Stop."

"So now what? I'm a little hungry, but not enough to face the restaurant crowds at six thirty on a Friday night."

Ugh. The wait would be two hours. At least. "Chinese?"

"Chinese. And June?"

"Yeah?"

He grabbed her hand and pulled her close, capturing her gaze. "We've done everything we can. It's in God's hands now."

40

July paced the kitchen. Shouldn't they have phoned by now? They'd never called with lab results after seven, and it was nearing six thirty.

"Come sit down. They'll call soon."

She frowned at Gareth. "What if they don't? They drew the blood this morning, surely they have it back by now? I don't want to wait until tomorrow. Or...gosh, would they make me wait until Monday?"

Gareth hit the mute button on the TV remote and patted the couch. "Sit. If they don't call, you'll go upstairs and take a pregnancy test. At this point, that ought to be just about as accurate as the blood test. I know they didn't want us to do that before hand, but we waited and followed their directions. If they can't get back to us in a timely manner, well...it won't hurt for you to pee on a stick."

July sank to the couch and dropped her head on his shoulder. "What if it's negative?"

He kissed the top of her head. "Then I guess we try again."

She twisted so she could see his face. He was willing to try again? That was new. "But I thought...the insurance coverage...the cost?"

"You're not ready to move to adoption yet. IVF isn't a guarantee—certainly not the first time or with the restrictions on the number of embryos we're allowing. So, if we need to try again we will."

Tears filled her eyes. "Oh, Gareth. Thank you."

"Hey." He tipped her chin up and held her gaze. "I love you."

She smiled and knuckled her eyes. Before she could speak, the phone rang. She froze. Her heart stopped mid-beat, her breath caught in her throat. Wide-eyed she stared at Gareth.

He picked up the handset and hit the talk button. "Hello...Yes, one moment."

He held out the phone, eyebrows lifted.

July pressed a hand to her heart and blew out a breath before taking the phone. "Hello...this is she...okay...Yes...Okay, thanks. Goodnight."

She pressed end and buried her face in her hands, tears spilling down her cheeks.

"Oh baby..."

She shook her head, gulping air. A sound, half-sob, half-laugh wrenched its way out of her. "I'm pregnant."

WANT A FREE BOOK?

If you enjoyed *Hope Deferred* and would like to read another book of mine, you can receive a free e-book simply by signing up for my newsletter here: http://bit.ly/2goAGvf

Keep reading for a sneak peek of the final book in the Remnants Series, Love Defined.

SNEAK PEEK OF LOVE DEFINED, REMNANTS BOOK 3

Love Defined
Remnants, Book 3

"So, I guess that's it?" A lead weight settled in July's stomach and she leaned against the headrest of the passenger seat and closed her eyes.

Gareth's fingers closed around hers and squeezed.

"I'm not wrong though, am I?" She cracked open an eye and held his gaze.

He shook his head. "No. Probably not."

She turned and stared out the window as Gareth backed out of the parking spot and pointed the car toward home. Two more miscarriages. This time twins. Five babies she'd never know this side of heaven and none to hold. Even the ever-confident-in-his-ability Dr. DiCola couldn't honestly recommend they try IVF for a third time. "What now?"

"I think we pray about what's next. There's no need to jump into anything, Jules."

Flashes of colorful spring blossoms blurred together as they sped around the Beltway. He was probably right... though the ache in her heart screamed for action. Maybe they should go ahead and try a third time anyway. What could it hurt? July opened her mouth to ask, then snapped it shut. There were entirely too many ways trying again could hurt. Another miscarriage topped that list, followed closely by the stress on their marriage. Another miscarriage... even if they didn't pursue IVF again, getting pregnant hadn't been her problem. The thought had been that IVF would make keeping the babies easier, plus speed up the timeframe since she was working with just one fallopian tube.

But it was likely she'd end up pregnant again if they didn't decide how to keep that from happening. She didn't want to go on the pill... would Gareth ever consider a vasectomy? Though that was so permanent. Maybe she needed to look into natural family planning more closely. June had mentioned it to her last year and it might just be the perfect solution.

July blew out a breath. "Can I be honest with you?"

Gareth glanced over, brow knitting. "Always."

"I'm not... I don't know how to pray about this." She twisted her fingers in her lap. She'd spent so much time praying for a child that now... what was left to say? God had given her children. Five of them. She just didn't get to keep them long. Had she not been specific enough in her prayers? Surely God knew she'd meant that she wanted to hold her babies, nurture them... watch them grow to adulthood?

"I haven't got an easy answer. I..." He sighed and flicked on the turn signal before pulling onto their exit. "Maybe we pray about that first? Ask Him to make His will clear to us. Because I'll be honest, I thought we were doing what He wanted us to do. I don't understand why we're in this situation any more than you do."

Gareth didn't have any answers either? How did that work? He was always the one who understood when things went wrong. Her heart began to race and she swallowed the bile that tried to inch up her throat. Was this what a panic attack felt like?

"Hey." Gareth pulled into the driveway and shifted into park. "It's going to be okay. We'll figure it out."

Right. Sure they would.

With a gentle finger, Gareth lifted her chin and held her gaze. "We will. I know it doesn't seem like it's possible. And I don't have any answers, but I have faith."

She offered a short nod. "Okay. You're right."

July took a deep breath in through her nose and held it. Her heart rate slowed as she let the air escape.

"That's my girl." He leaned over and kissed her. "Come on, let's go in. You can put your feet up. Maybe we'll find something good on TV."

July crept downstairs to the office and prodded her computer awake. How was Gareth able to sleep? Every time she closed her eyes, babies floated through her head. The images wouldn't leave her alone while she'd flopped from one position to another, so she'd given in and gotten up. Three girls and two boys. There was no way to know for certain that those genders were right. But they felt right. And there was no point dwelling on it.

She hovered the mouse over her social media shortcut. Did she really want to see everyone's happy family photos? Or read about how terrible their jobs were? Not really. She opened her email instead. June had written—probably asking for an update. A lump lodged in her throat. That could wait 'til tomorrow. Her gaze traveled to the list of adoption resources she'd collected in a draft email. Butterflies swirled in her stomach as she began clicking the links, opening each in a new tab. There was no point in putting it off any longer.

Gareth had kept up his end of the deal, now she had to keep hers.

Okay... what had June said was step one? Decide between international or domestic, right? July blew out a breath. Where did you even start trying to figure that out? She clicked on the tab for an international adoption agency. The words swam across the screen. She blinked furiously to clear the tears that pooled in her eyes. Why wasn't "neither" an option? Because she'd promised Gareth, that's why.

She slid open the middle desk drawer and rooted around for a pen and pad of paper. She'd approach this logically. And maybe, just maybe, having lists would prove once and for all that this wasn't the right choice for them. She ripped off the top sheet and wrote "International" across the top before drawing a line down the center of the page. She labeled one side "Pros" and the other "Cons." Then she repeated the process on another sheet of paper, except the label at the top said "Domestic."

Pen in hand, she began to read.

THANK YOU!

I hope you enjoyed *Hope Deferred*! I need to ask you a favor. Would you help others enjoy this book too?

Recommend it. Please help other readers find this book by recommending it to friends in person and on social media.

Review it. Reviews can be tough to come by these days. You, the reader, have the power to make or break a book. Loved it, hated it – I'd just enjoy your feedback. Please tell other readers what you thought about this book by reviewing it on any major retailer or social media site.

Thank you so much for reading *Hope Deferred* and for spending time with me.

AUTHOR'S NOTE

Books don't just happen. There are so many people who have made it possible for me to get words onto pages. My incredible editor, Lynellen Perry. My husband who watches the kids when I need "just five more minutes". My critique partner, Janice, and beta readers Megan and Rachel. Thank you!

Thanks also to you, the reader. While I do derive a tiny bit of joy just knowing my books are published, the majority of my delight comes from knowing that my words have given someone else an enjoyable respite from reality.

Above all, thanks to God for giving me ideas that turn into stories that turn into books. Without His seed of inspiration and continued encouragement, I'd be adrift.

RESOURCES

Resolve.org is the home of the National Infertility Association. Their website has a wealth of useful information.

Though rather old (2004), you may be interested in "The Infertility Companion: Hope and Help for Couples Facing Infertility" by Sandra L. Glahn and William R. Cutrer, and endorsed by the Christian Medical Association.

A newer book (2010) is "Outside the Womb: Moral Guidance for Assisted Reproduction" by Scott Rae and Joy Riley, MD.

Christianity Today magazine has a good article from 2010, titled "Frozen Embryos: Biotech's Hidden Dilemma" which documents the opinions of three experts. http://www.christianitytoday.com/ct/2010/july/25.46.html

Though not specifically infertility related, the best book I've ever read on the subject of the problem of evil is Randy Alcorn's *If God is Good*. If this is something you struggle with, it's a worthwhile investment of your time.

DISCUSSION QUESTIONS

1. When do you believe life begins? At conception or another time? How has that affected your thoughts about in-vitro fertilization (or other medically assisted means of reproduction)?

2. Toby thinks through the following: *The doctor had mentioned using donor eggs and doing IVF. Did she want to consider that? The idea made him squirm. Didn't it, effectively, mean June would carry a child he made with another woman? Even if the process took place in a lab... he suppressed a shudder. Maybe it worked for other people, that was fine, but it wasn't something he wanted to do.* What are your thoughts on donor eggs and donor sperm?

3. June asks Toby what he thinks about asking July to make extra embroys that could then be implanted in June to raise as her own children. What are your thoughts about this idea?

4. June says, "We're raised to believe that children are a blessing from God. The ideal Christian woman is painted as one who's at home with a brood of kids,

teaching them, loving them, raising them up as the next generation. Even if she continues to work, the career woman is a mother first if she's a good Christian wife." What's your reaction?

5. If you were going to give July and Gareth marriage advice, what would you tell them?

6. How did your parents fight? What things do you do similarly and differently when you fight with your spouse?

7. Do you think pre-marital counseling should include discussions about the details of infertility treatments and adoption?

8. July says, "I'd be on board with adding to our family through adoption. But I want at least one of our kids to be wholly ours, not some kind of long-term mission project." What's your reaction to that?

9. In your opinion, does June's failure to respond to medication make her situation easier or harder?

10. How do you think you would react if your child was unable to conceive grandchildren?

11. Do you believe that children need to be raised in ethnically similar households? Why or why not?

ABOUT THE AUTHOR

Elizabeth Maddrey is a semi-reformed computer geek and homeschooling mother of two who lives in the suburbs of Washington D.C. When she isn't writing, Elizabeth is a voracious consumer of books. She loves to write about Christians who struggle through their lives, dealing with sin and receiving God's grace on their way to their own romantic happily ever after.

Visit her website at www.ElizabethMaddrey.com